Franck Barrington

Kansas day

Containing a brief history of Kansas and a collection by Kansas authors

Franck Barrington

Kansas day
Containing a brief history of Kansas and a collection by Kansas authors

ISBN/EAN: 9783337280239

Printed in Europe, USA, Canada, Australia, Japan

Cover: Foto ©Andreas Hilbeck / pixelio.de

More available books at **www.hansebooks.com**

A BRIEF HISTORY OF KANSAS,

AND A

COLLECTION BY KANSAS AUTHORS,

WITH OTHER MISCELLANEOUS MATTER PERTAINING TO KANSAS.

By F. H. BARRINGTON,

PRINCIPAL OF SCHOOLS, McCRACKEN, KANSAS.

"Then we should gather, I think, what may be called 'home books;' books about America; about the United States of America; about Kansas, the heart of America; books written by Americans about America—about Kansas. . . Gather such books that there may grow in young hearts that passionate attachment to our home and country—one's own visible and actual country"
— N. L. PRENTIS.

TOPEKA, KANSAS: -
GEO. W. CRANE & COMPANY.
1892.

DEDICATION.

TO the thousands of bright-eyed, rosy-cheeked boys and girls who answer to roll-call in our Kansas schools, and to the hundreds of devoted Kansas teachers who are training these boys and girls to a true conception of American citizenship and to a deeper love for our great State, this little book is dedicated.

THE AUTHOR.

PREFACE.

THE plan of this little book grew out of the need of such a work, experienced by the author during his labors in the public schools of Kansas. For several years the writer has been gathering scrap-book collections pertaining to Kansas lore, and has successfully used them in general exercises, and in celebrating our State's birthday, with a view to familiarizing pupils with a few leading events and principal characters connected with the history of the State—a history containing all the varying shades, from darkest midnight to brightest noonday.

The recent increase of interest among Kansas people upon the subject of government, especially that of our State, is a hopeful sign. The unparalleled political wave which two years ago swept over Kansas, burying from view more than fourscore thousand of the dominant party, demonstrated as never before the power and majesty of a nineteenth century republic. A better knowledge of our political institutions can but lead to better citizenship; in short, good citizenship is impossible unless the people understand the government under which they live.

So closely is Kansas history interwoven with that of the

National Government, the transition from one to the other is natural and easy; but owing to the scarcity of Kansas books in the average Kansas home and in the schools, the author has found the teaching of Kansas History a laborious task, though a pleasant one. In this little work the compiler has kept in view the fact that boys and girls must be led — must be interested in the study — hence the plan : A brief mention of the leading events in the history of the State, with marginal notes for reference readings contained in the body of the work. Many of these have been selected to add interest to some point in history, or for the sentiment or facetiæ contained rather than for any literary merit.they possess.

With this explanation we trust *litterateurs* will "pass our imperfections by" and search out the beauties of thought and expression contained in other and better productions, with which we think many of these pages are replete.

Though the book is intended especially for use in the public schools, the writer believes that it will find a welcome nook in the home library of the Kansas girl or boy, and that even older heads may select something from within these covers that will prove entertaining and furnish some food for thought.

While the reader is studying these pages, he will not only learn something of the history of our great State, but at the same time make the acquaintance of some of her best writers.

Hence the author believes that many of these selections

could be successfully used for supplementary reading in schools and institutes.

But little of originality is claimed by the author of this work. As before stated, much of the matter herein contained has been collected from scraps and notes, made from time to time during several years past, and for this reason quotation-marks and names of authors may be lacking because it was impossible to place them accurately.

The author has derived much assistance from Wilder's Annals, and the Histories of Andreas, Spring, and Robinson; also Frost's Kansas Collection, and Mrs. Allerton's poems, to which the writer has had free forage.

Special thanks are due the officers of the State Historical Society, and to Miss Hattie Horner, Mr. T. E. Dewey, Mrs. May Belleville Brown, and Honorable B. W. Woodward, for encouraging words, kind criticism, and valuable suggestions.

This book has been prepared amid the many cares and duties attendant upon the principalship of a village school; hence, because of its many literary imperfections, we expect it to find little favor with the ever-present severe literary critic, but we hope to find its friends among the earnest teachers and the thoughtful parents who value the awakening of a single thought leading to an appreciation

"Of what we fought to build in bleeding Kansas' days."

THE AUTHOR.

CONTENTS.

PART I.

KANSAS HISTORY.

CHAPTER I.—EARLY EXPLORERS AND EXPLORATIONS.

Spanish—French—American, ... 15

CHAPTER II.—SLAVERY AGITATION.

Kansas a Highway—Missouri Compromise—Omnibus Bill—Kansas
and Nebraska Bill, ... 22

CHAPTER III.—THE CONTEST IN KANSAS.

Moves and Countermoves—Emigrant Aid Society—Blue Lodges
and Law-and-Order Societies—Governor Reeder—First Elec-
tion—Second Territorial Election—First Territorial Legislature
—First Free-State Convention—October Elections—Topeka
Convention—Governors Woodson and Shannon—Beecher
Bibles—Climax Reached, ... 25

CHAPTER IV.—WAKARUSA WAR.

Rescue of Branson—Raid on Lawrence—Murder of Barber—Results of the Wakarusa War, ... 32

CHAPTER V.—PRO-SLAVERY AND FREE-STATE DEPREDATIONS.

Jones Wounded—Territorial Indictments—Second Raid on Lawrence—Other Depredations—Free-State Men Retaliate, . . . 36

CHAPTER VI.—MORE FIGHTING.

Pottawatomie Massacre—Black Jack—Dispersing the Invaders—
Kansas Aid Society—Agitations in the South—Battle of
Franklin—Second Battle of Franklin—Fort Saunders Captured
—Fort Titus—Treaty of Peace—Governor Shannon Resigns—
Battle of Osawatomie—John Brown Monument—Sequel to the
Battle of Osawatomie—Movement Against Lecompton, . . . 39

(7)

8 CONTENTS.

CHAPTER VII.— GOVERNOR GEARY'S ADMINISTRATION.

Geary's Plans — Battle of Hickory Point — Third Attempt to Destroy Lawrence — First Thanksgiving Proclamation — Topeka Legislature — The Territorial Legislature, ... 46

CHAPTER VIII.— A CHAPTER IN POLITICS.

Acting Governors Woodson and Stanton — Governor Walker — The Elections — The Lecompton Convention — Resignation of Walker and Removal of Stanton — First Free-State Legislature — Vote on the Lecompton Constitution — Vote on Constitution and State Officers — The Disposal of the Lecompton Constitution — Last of the Topeka Legislature — Third Territorial Legislature — More Conventions and Constitutions, ... 50

CHAPTER IX.— WAR IN THE SOUTHEAST.

Battle of Middle Creek — Captain Clarke's Exploits — James Montgomery — Marais des Cygnes — John Brown again in Kansas — John Brown's Famous Parallels, ... 56

CHAPTER X.— KANSAS BECOMES A STATE.

First Republican Party in Kansas — Governors Denver, Medary — Kansas Famine 1860 — Kansas Admitted — How the News was Received — State Seal — Origin of Name and Meaning of Motto, 60

CHAPTER XI.— KANSAS DURING THE CIVIL WAR.

Lawrence Raid, 1863 — Price Raid — Battles of Lexington, Big Blue, and Westport — Pursuit of Price, ... 63

CHAPTER XII.— INDIAN WARS.

Pawnees and Omahas — Cheyennes, Arapahoes and Kiowas — Raid of 1868 — General Sulley's Campaign — Nineteenth Kansas Cavalry — Battle of the Wachita — Close of the War, ... 67

CHAPTER XIII.— IN MEMORIAM.

James Montgomery — James H. Lane — John Brown, ... 70

CHAPTER XIV.— PEACE.

Kansas State Historical Society — State Reform School — State Industrial School for Girls — State Normal (frontispiece) — Kansas State University — Railroads — Growth in Population and Wealth — Agriculture — Churches — Public Schools — Temperance, ... 74

PART II.

A COLLECTION FROM KANSAS AUTHORS.

A Kansas Wish, ... Charles Moreau Harger, . 85
A Kansas Collection, ... J. W. D. Anderson, . . . 86
Now I Lay Me, ... Anonymous, ... 88
Kansas-Day Song, ... Laura E. Newell, . . . 90
The Kansas Dugout, ... E. F. Ware, ... 91
Mis' Smith, ... A. B. Paine, ... 92
Kansas Courage, ... C. F. Scott, ... 93
The Gates Ajar, ... Albert Bigelow Paine, . 95
Hickorye Creek Logic, ... Helianthus Annuus, . . 96
Little Things, ... Mrs. Allerton, ... 96
Judge Brewer on Kansas, ... 97
Pawpaws Ripe, ... Sol. Miller, ... 98
Kansas — A Recitation, ... Maggie A. Kilmer, . . . 102
Sunflower Song, ... Anonymous, ... 103
A Tribute to John Brown, . . . J. G. Waters, ... 105
A Farmer's Wife, ... Ewing Herbert, ... 105
Sing a Song of Kansas, ... Emporia Republican, . . 106
Kansas, ... W. F. Craig, ... 107
Resubmission, ... Mrs. Emma P. Seabury, . 108
John Brown's Last Speech, ... 111
Don't You Tell, ... Mrs. Allerton, ... 112
The Sod School-House (Illustrated), C. M. Harger, ... 113
The World a School, ... Noble L. Prentis, . . . 114
John Brown, ... Eugene F. Ware, ... 116
The Coyote, ... Jas. W. Steele, ... 118
Quivera — Kansas, ... Eugene Ware, ... 120
The Trail of '49, ... Mrs. Allerton, ... 122
To Kansas, ... A. G. Canfield, ... 124
God Save Our Town, ... N. L. Prentis, ... 126
Kansas — For a Picture, ... Florence L. Snow, . . . 127
The State Reform School, ... W. E. Fagan, ... 128
Kansas — Retrospective, ... Geo. A. Root, ... 130
Death of the Spanish Three Hun-
    dred, ... John Madden, ... 132
Original Package, ... Emma P. Seabury, . . . 134
The Whistling Engineer, ... J. M. Cavaness, ... 135

JOHN BROWN'S PARALLELS,	John Brown,	136
THE CYCLONE OF MAY 27, 1892,	T. S. Brown,	138
TTE OLD SOD SHANTY ON THE CLAIM (Illustrated),	Anonymous,	140
THE WILD SUNFLOWER,	Albert Bigelow Paine,	142
HOW WE TOOK TITUS,	B. W. Woodward,	143
A DREAM OF THE SEA,	A. B. Paine,	147
A BORDER MEMORY,	Florence L. Snow,	148
KANSAS WEATHER,	C. S. White,	152
THE FIELDS OF KANSAS,	Ellen P. Allerton,	153
WHEN THE SUNFLOWERS BLOOM,	A. B. Paine,	155
A MOUNTAIN INCIDENT,	Mrs. S. N. Wood,	156
GOVERNOR REEDER'S SPEECH,	A. H. Reeder,	158
THE KANSAS INDIAN'S LAMENT,	Thomas Brower Peacock,	160
LAWRENCE RAID,	Ellen Patton,	162
GOLDEN ROD IN KANSAS,	Ad H. Gibson,	163
TO A KANSAS REDBIRD,	Ad H. Gibson,	164
WALLS OF CORN,	Mrs. Allerton,	165
BEAUTIFUL THINGS,	Mrs. Allerton,	167
IN THE EAR, OR IN THE JUG,	John P. St. John,	168
BLEEDING KANSAS DAYS,	Carl Brann,	171
TAKE HEART,	Ad H. Gibson,	173
THE MODEL OLD COUPLE,	Sol. Miller,	174
A CHURCH BELL OF MANHATTAN,	Ida A. Ahlborn,	176
THE REUNION AT WIDDY MACHREE'S,	Maggie MacKilmer,	177
KANSAS,	A. A. B. Cavaness,	179
JAMES MONTGOMERY,	Joel Moody,	181
SELECTIONS FROM TWO PICTURES,	J. Lee Knight,	181
JULY FOURTH,	A. A. B. Cavaness,	183
THE INTERREGNUM,	Will A. White,	184
THE ATHENA OF AMERICAN STATES,	John A. Martin,	187
OPPORTUNITY,	John J. Ingalls,	188
KANSAS, 1874–1884,	Hattie Horner,	188
THE STORY OF THE FLAG,	Edward T. Barber,	191
EARLY REMINISCENCES,	Mrs. Sarah L. Pinkston,	194
KANSAS—A SONG,	Mary Ray McIntire,	196
KANSAS; ITS PAST, PRESENT, AND FUTURE,	Laura E. Newell,	198
THE NATAL HOUR,	Joel Moody,	199
THE HOME,	Joel Moody,	200
AD ASTRA PER ASPERA,	Laura E. Newell,	201

KANSAS, ... Anonymous, ... 202
THE OLD SOLDIER, ... Geo. R. Peck, ... 203
THE SUNFLOWERS OF KANSAS, ... Anonymous, ... 204
THE REPORTER AND THE TRAVELING
    MAN, ... Troy Chief, ... 204
THE HOMES OF KANSAS, ... Sol. Miller, ... 206
SOL. MILLER AS A POET, ... Ewing Herbert, . . . 208
THE TEACHER, ... B. W. Allsworth, . . . 209
ON THE FARM, ... Mrs. Allerton, ... 210
ONLY A NEGRO, ... Carl Brann, ... 212
TELL ME, YE KANSAS WINDS, ... J. M. Cavaness, . . . 214
DON'T WAKEN THE BABY, ... Mrs. S. N. Wood, . . . 215
MY AMBITION, ... Mrs. Allerton, ... 216
CHILDHOOD, ... Ironquill, ... 217
PILGRIM BARD, ... Scott Cummins, . . . 218
TO-DAY, ... Ironquill, ... 218
"OLD JIM," . . . . F. H. B., ... 219
QUOTATIONS, ... 226
KANSAS SYMPOSIUM, ... 229

PART III.

MISCELLANEOUS.

KANSAS, ... National Tribune, . . . 239
LE MARAIS DU CYGNE, ... Whittier, ... 240
THE BURIAL OF BARBER, ... Whittier, ... 242
THE KANSAS EMIGRANT'S SONG, . . . Whittier, ... 243
K T DID, ... Vanity Fair, ... 245
PROPHETIC WORDS OF SUMNER, . . . Chas. Sumner, ... 246
WORDS OF WILKES, OF SOUTH CARO-
    LINA, ... Warren Wilkes, ... 247
EMERSON ON KANSAS, ... R. W. Emerson, ... 247
ORIGINAL JOHN BROWN SONG, ... Anonymous, ... 248
A CALL TO KANSAS, ... Lucy Larcom, ... 249
POETIC DESCRIPTION OF KANSAS, . . H. W. Longfellow, . . . 252

PART I.

KANSAS HISTORY.

CHAPTER I.

SPANISH EXPLORATIONS.—The first clear and authentic account of the territory now included in Kansas is that of the Spaniard Francisco Vasquez de Coronado, a companion of Cortez, the conqueror of Mexico. Rumors of the country of Quivera* were probably first set afloat by one Cabeza de Vaca, a member of the ill-fated Narvez expedition. De Vaca and three others, after a six-years imprisonment on an island near the mouth of the Mississippi, made their escape in September, 1534, and passing through northern Alabama, turned westward, "crossed the river from the north," (the Mississippi,) and after eighteen months of weary toil, dangers, and privations, arrived at a Spanish settlement in Mexico. The Spaniards, whose greedy ears were ever ready to credit the most visionary stories, received with wonder and enthusiasm the tales of De Vaca and his companions, of wonderful cities, whose inhabitants lived in seven-story buildings, dined from dishes of solid gold, and were awakened from sleep by the chime of golden bells, which hung from the branches of the trees.

Coronado sent out from Mexico two expeditions to explore and subjugate portions of this fabulous country. A leader of one of these expeditions brought to Coronado an Indian called "Il Turco" (The Turk), who, fearful that

---

* "Quivera," Part 2. (15)

the invaders would lay waste the whole country, and murder and enslave his people, determined to play upon the avarice of the Spaniards by enlarging upon the reports already in circulation, and lead them into a far-off desert, where he hoped the horses, which they so much feared, would die of thirst and heat, and without which the Spaniards would be unable to return and do them harm. The Turk described his home, Quivera, as lying many miles to the north, with its river seven miles wide, in which swam fishes as large as horses.

Coronado started from the Rio Grande May 5th, 1541, with three hundred followers, mostly Spanish noblemen, and entered the mighty plains and sandy heaths of New Mexico and Kansas.

Here we note the first account of the Indians of the plains, who depended entirely on the chase for sustenance, and of the cibola (bison), great crooked-back cattle, "foul and fierce beasts of countenance and form of body." In thirty-seven days they arrived at the Arkansas river. Here, against the protestations of his soldiers, because of scarcity of provisions and the hopelessness of the outlook, Coronado with thirty soldiers, mostly mounted, and a few additional Indians, determined to push his search to the northward in search of Quivera, the main part of the command returning to their camp on the Rio Grande.

Coronado's exact route through Kansas is mainly conjecture. He doubtless passed through that portion of the State now comprising Barber, Kingman, Reno, Harvey, McPherson, Marion, Dickinson, Davis, Riley, Pottawatomie, and Nemaha counties.

Historians locate Quivera between the Platte and Kansas rivers, and between longitude 95 and 98.

Coronado, in his description of Quivera, writes, in sub-
stance, that he reached the 40th parallel, 3,200 miles from
Mexico, and that the soil is black, and is adapted to the
productions of Spain, including all kinds of fruits. The
surface is described as being free from mountains, there
being some hills and plains, interspersed with large and
small streams of water.

This first exploration of Kansas achieved nothing of importance. Well-nigh two hundred years elapse before the
European again turns his attention to this land.

The false Il Turco — false to his enemies, that he might
be faithful to his people — acknowledged his deception,
and was summarily put to death.

"In 1721 a colony of 300 people left Santa Fé to plant
a Spanish outpost in Kansas. The company was composed of men with their families and stock, and was in
charge of a friar of the order of St. Dominic, whose holy
mission was to Christianize the savages. Every man,
woman and child was massacred by the inhuman barbari-
ans of the plains."[*]

FRENCH EXPLORATIONS.—Kansas was originally a part of
the Louisiana Purchase. It extended from Missouri westward to the top of the Rocky Mountains, and northward
from the 37th to the 40th parallel, covering an area of
more than 125,000 square miles.

In 1719 M. du Tissenet — sometimes written Dutisne or
Duquesne — under the orders of the governor of Louisiana,
explored Kansas westward to the head-waters of the Smoky
Hill. On the 27th of September, in what is now western
Kansas, he erected a cross, thus claiming the territory in
the name of France.

---

[*] "Death of the Spanish Three Hundred," Part 2.

M. du Tissenet was the first to mention the abundance of salt, and the first to give definite information of Indian tribes.

In 1722–23 the French erected a fort near the junction of the Osage with the Missouri river, called Fort Orleans. The commander, Du Bourgmont, during succeeding years, made extended tours into Kansas, made friends with the Indians, which however was of short duration, for in 1725 the Kansas aborigines captured the fort and massacred the garrison— not one escaping to tell how it was accomplished.

This ended the attempts of the French to occupy this territory. Its history is shrouded in obscurity till, in 1803, it was again brought into prominence through the purchase from Napoleon, of France, by the United States, "that vast territory vaguely described as the country drained by the Mississippi and its tributaries."

AMERICAN EXPLORATIONS.—*Lewis and Clark.*— In 1804– 1806, Lewis and Clark crossed to the Pacific ocean and returned, bringing to light the first definite knowledge of the topography of the country, its resources and climate.

Captain Pike's Expedition. — In 1806, Captain Pike, with a small army of 23 white men and 50 Indians, started from near the mouth of the Missouri, following it to the mouth of the Osage river, thence up the Osage to its source, crossing the head of the Neosho, thence to the mouth of the Saline.

Mr. Pike says: "On our march we were continually passing through large herds of buffaloes, elk, and cabrie, and I have no doubt but one hunter could support two hundred men."

Captain Pike then turned to the southward, after visit-

ing various heads of Indian tribes. Reaching the Arkansas river; he divided his force, sending a party by boat
down the river, while he, taking the remaining force,
started on his march westward. On November 14th he
discovered the peak which bears his name. After marching eight days, he concluded to camp his men and with
only three companions visit, and if practicable ascend, the
"blue mountain." They reached the foot of the mountain
on the evening of the second day. The account of the
ascent of Pike's Peak we give in his own words:

"*Wednesday, 26th November.*—Expecting to return to
our camp that evening, we left all our blankets and provisions at the foot of the mountain; killed a deer of a new
species, and hung his skin on a tree, with some meat. We
commenced ascending; found the way very difficult, being
obliged to climb up rocks sometimes almost perpendicular;
and after marching all day we encamped in a cave, without blankets, victuals, or water. We had a fine, clear sky,
whilst it was snowing at the bottom. On the side of the
mountain we found only yellow and pitch pine; some distance up we saw buffalo; and higher still, the new species
of deer, and pheasants.

"*Thursday, 27th November.*—Arose hungry, thirsty, and
extremely sore, from the unevenness of the rocks on which
we had lain all night; but were amply compensated for
our toil by the sublimity of the prospects below. The unbounded prairie was overhung with clouds, which appeared
like the ocean in a storm, wave piled on wave, and foam-
ing, whilst the sky over our heads was perfectly clear.
Commenced our march up the mountain, and in about one
hour arrived at the summit of this chain; here we found
the snow middle deep, and discovered no sign of beast or

bird inhabiting this region. The thermometer, which stood at nine degrees above zero at the foot of the mountain, here fell to four degrees below. The summit of the Grand Peak, which was entirely bare of vegetation, and covered with snow, now appeared at a distance of fifteen or sixteen miles from us, and as high again as that we had ascended. It would have taken a whole day's march to have arrived at its base, while I believe no human being could have ascended to its summit. This, with the condition of my soldiers, who had only light overalls on, and no stockings, and were every way ill provided to endure the inclemency of this region, the bad prospects of killing anything to subsist on, with the further detention of two or three days which it must occasion, determined us to return. The clouds from below had now ascended the mountain and entirely enveloped the summit, on which rest eternal snows. We descended by a long, deep ravine, with much less difficulty than we had contemplated. Found all our baggage safe, but the provisions all destroyed. It began to snow, and we sought shelter under the side of a projecting rock, where we all four made a meal on one partridge and a pair of deer's ribs, which the ravens had left us, being the first food we had eaten for forty-eight hours." [*Andreas' History.*]

Captain Pike, in giving his impression of the country, says: "On the rivers, Kansas, La Platte, Arkansas and their tributaries, it appears to me to be only possible to introduce a limited population. The wood would not be sufficient for a moderate population more than fifteen years. The borders of the Arkansas may be termed the paradise terrestrial of our territories for the wandering savages. I believe that here are buffalo, elk and deer sufficient, if used without waste, to feed all the savages of the United States territory for one century."

Within the limits described by Captain Pike there now exist (1892) nearly three million inhabitants. The savages, the elk, deer, and buffalo, have departed; while the golden wheat-fields and the rustling leaves of corn attest the prosperity of the people.

Yet, notwithstanding Captain Pike's evident failure as a prophet, it by no means detracts from the accurate and valuable information gained by his travels, and which he so graphically imparted to posterity.

CHAPTER II.

KANSAS A HIGHWAY.—"With the establishment of American occupancy an era of migration set in through Kansas toward the Pacific slope—a migration at first slender, capricious, and without system, but acquiring ultimately volume, method and persistence sufficient to imprint clear-cut trails sheer across the mighty plains.* Traders, eager to seize upon new and inviting avenues of commerce; travelers, ambitious to compel the half-unknown world beyond the Missouri to yield up its secrets; Kearny's soldiers, with greedy eyes fixed on New Mexico; Mormons, fleeing into the wilderness before the wrath of civilization; gold-hunters, aflame with visions of sudden wealth among the mines of California;—such was the heterogeneous, intermittent mob that trooped across Kansas during the years immediately preceding the Kansas-Nebraska legislation." [*Spring.*]

THE MISSOURI COMPROMISE.—Ever since the formation of the Federal constitution the question of slavery had been agitated in Congress. When the bill for the admission of Missouri came before Congress, a memorable discussion arose, lengthy and violent. Northern members opposed the extension of slavery on moral and political grounds. The Southern members, having great interests invested in slave labor, and advocating the doctrine of

---

* "The Trail of '49," Part 2.

(22)

"State rights," denied the right of the General Government, under the constitution, to interfere with affairs of the several States, holding that the people of a State should decide whether slavery should or should not exist within her borders.

At this juncture — 1820 — Southern champions introduced the bill known as the Missouri Compromise, which provided that Missouri should be admitted as a slave State, and that thereafter slavery should forever be prohibited north of 36° 30'. The territory south of that line was to be opened to slavery or freedom, as the people should choose.

THE OMNIBUS BILL. — The momentous question of slavery was destined to again become the bone of contention in American politics. The question of the admission of California, and other subjects either directly or indirectly related to slavery, for months agitated Congress and the people at large, till there were grave fears of the disruption of the Union.

At length, in January, 1850, Henry Clay comes to the front with his compromise measure — the omnibus bill, which was the means by which a final general conflict between the North and South was postponed ten years. By this compromise California was admitted as a free State. The boundary-line between Texas and New Mexico was settled; Utah and New Mexico were organized as Territories without the question of slavery. Slavery was abolished in the District of Columbia, and the fugitive slave law was passed, providing for the capture and delivery of runaway slaves who had escaped from the South to the North.

THE KANSAS AND NEBRASKA BILL. — The legislative event

of Pierce's administration was the passage of the Kansas and Nebraska bill.

In 1853 the massive brain of that orator and statesman, Stephen A. Douglas, evolved the question — or mistake, if you please — which quenched the star of his political destiny, and deluged the Territory of Kansas in blood. This measure left the question whether slavery should or should not exist in Kansas and Nebraska, to the settlers of the soil.

"One volume in the Kansas Historical Society's library contains eighty speeches* on this bill by eighty different members at one session, including six messages from the President. The exciting debate lasted four months. At one time Congress had a two-months contest for Speaker, in which over a hundred ballots were taken. Both parties looked upon Kansas with absorbing interest.† President Pierce signed the bill in 1854."

---

* "Prophetic Words of Sumner," Part 3.

† "Words of Warren Wilkes, of South Carolina," Part 3.

CHAPTER III.

THE CONTEST IN KANSAS.

MOVES AND COUNTER-MOVES.—The steps to make Kansas a State were: to elect a Territorial Legislature, which might arrange a constitutional convention to frame a constitution for or against slavery. Votes, then, were the prerequisite consideration. People flocked in from the Southern States to carry the election.

Missouri, with her slaves worth thirty millions of dollars, took an active part, to the end that slavery might be perpetuated in the sister republic. Hundreds pushed across the border and seized upon the best lands by simply marking their claim upon trees or laying a foundation consisting of four logs or rails.

The pro-slavery towns of Kickapoo, Atchison—named in honor of Senator Atchison, of Missouri, a prominent pro-slavery leader in Kansas—Leavenworth, on the Missouri, and the historic town, Lecompton, the political headquarters of the Pro-Slavery party, sprang up.

Those who opposed the extension of slavery formed immigration societies throughout the North, furnishing free transportation to those who were willing to throw their votes and their lives into the balance. Civil war was inevitable, and it came in some of its worst aspects. Volumes might be filled with reminiscences of that terrible conflict. The stories of indiscriminate slaughter of human beings, of homes made desolate, of hair-breadth escapes, of deeds of daring, patriotism, and personal sacrifice, find no parallel in the history of any other State in the Union.*

THE EMIGRANT AID SOCIETY.—This society, having for its object the settlement of Kansas by Free-State men, owed largely its origin and success to Eli Thayer, of Worcester, Massachusetts, who preached the tireless gospel of organized emigration† with tireless and successful enthusiasm, while Amos A. Lawrence discharged the burdensome but all-important duties of treasurer. John Carter Brown, of Rhode Island, was chosen president, and with these officers and twenty directors, more than fourteen thousand souls were enabled to reach Kansas over the route of the Emigrant Aid Society.‡ One hundred and fifty thousand dollars was collected and disbursed — a sum in itself small, but large in that many other organizations in the North were encouraged to follow this feasible plan of dealing with a grave political problem.

The man of all others in Kansas who possessed the confidence of the Emigrant Aid Society was Dr. Charles Robinson. He had, in 1849, crossed the Territory of Kansas on a trip overland to California, and had noted its many advantages. His name is closely interwoven with the history of his State.

In August, 1854, C. H. Branscomb conducted the first party, twenty-nine in number, to the present site of Lawrence — so named in honor of the treasurer of the association.

Wabaunsee, Osawatomie, Manhattan,§ Topeka, and other anti-slavery towns were planted.

---

* "Bleeding Kansas Days," Part 2.
† "A Call to Kansas," Part 3.
‡ "The Kansas Emigrant's Song," Part 3.
§ "A Church-Bell of Manhattan," Part 2.

It must not be understood that organized emigration alone took part in the great movement to make Kansas a free State. Settlers had preceded the first colony to the vicinity of Lawrence. The most noted of these perhaps, were S. N. Wood, Josiah Miller, J. A. Wakefield, and others,* who took an active part in the great contest.

BLUE LODGES AND "LAW-AND-ORDER" SOCIETIES.— Secret societies under the above names were organized in 1854, promising protection to every one except abolitionists; —an "abolitionist" was defined as being anyone from north of Mason and Dixon's line.

GOVERNOR REEDER.— Andrew H. Reeder, the first Governor of Kansas Territory, arrived on Kansas soil in October, 1854. It is said that his pledge—referring to the spirit of violence in the Territory—"I will crush it out or sacrifice myself in the effort," failed to elicit applause from the rank pro-slavery element to whom it was addressed.

FIRST ELECTION.— Little interest was taken by actual settlers in the election of a Delegate to Congress on November 29, 1854; yet the Missourians, more than 1700 strong, distributing themselves throughout the different election districts, cast their ballots for J. W. Whitfield.

SECOND TERRITORIAL ELECTION.— Both parties realized the importance of securing the Legislature which was to be chosen on the 30th of March, 1855. Pro-slavery orators were abroad denouncing "abolitionists" in no delicate terms. Those residents in Missouri who could not personally supervise the election in Kansas furnished money, arms, and ammunition. The Missourians appeared at the

* "Early Reminiscences," Part 2.

several voting-places in wagons and on horseback, armed with guns, pistols, and knives.

At some points they compelled the election judges to resign. The Missouri hordes and their allies swept all before them. According to the census taken by the authorities in February, there were 4,908 illegal votes cast. The facts of the invasion were known in the Territory immediately after the election, and the newspapers soon published them to the world. The Pro-Slavery party boasted of their achievement in electing a pro-slavery Legislature. The Free-State men of Kansas were of course indignant.

Andreas, page 97, quotes the New York *Tribune* to show the sentiment of the press:

"The great battle between Freedom and Slavery is gradually approaching; yet the country is everywhere quiet, and the public tranquility is undisturbed. Not even the distant rumble of the tempest is heard. The little cloud that denotes it hovers only over a handful of people in the far West. In Kansas alone exists the speck that foreshadows the coming storm. Kansas has been invaded by slavery. It is threatened with the unending curses of that institution. A country large enough for a kingdom is here to be wrested from the possession of the free States and blackened with African bondage. . . . The free Territories of this Union are the possessions it covets, and it has marshaled its forces and armed its mercenary hosts to conquer them. The battle is begun."

First Territorial Legislature.—This body assembled at Pawnee, July 2, 1855, and in four days it adjourned to meet again at Shawnee Mission, Johnson county, in eastern Kansas, near the Missouri line, without consulting Governor Reeder, who now took this ground as a reason for repudiating the Legislature. The laws enacted were copied from the slave statutes of Missouri. The Free-State men realized that the Legislature would be supported by the General Government and the Territorial judiciary.

FIRST FREE-STATE CONVENTION.—The first Free-State delegate convention met at Big Springs, Douglas county, though previous to this there had been two Free-State gatherings at Lawrence. These, however, looked more to the enunciation of principles than to immediate action, and simply opened the way for more efficient work at the delegate convention at Big Springs. This convention recommended the framing of a constitution and the formation of a State government; and for member of Congress nominated Governor Reeder, who had been removed from office. Mr. Reeder responded in a ringing speech.* "The work of the convention closed in an enthusiastic furor of cheers, handshakings, swearing, and tears." At the first meeting at Lawrence, James H. Lane, one of the great leaders of the Free-State party, made his first Free-State speech.

OCTOBER ELECTIONS.—On October 1st the Pro-Slavery party elected J. W. Whitfield. Out of the 2,721 votes cast, only 17 were scattering. On October 9th Reeder received all the Free-State votes polled, viz., 2,849. Reeder unsuccessfully contested the election. Whitfield was declared elected.

TOPEKA CONVENTION.—The constitutional convention, held at Topeka, October 23d, lasted eighteen days. It framed a constitution containing the following salient features: Adopting the boundaries of the Kansas and Nebraska bill; located the capital at Topeka; and prohibited slav-

---

* Speech of Andrew H. Reeder, Part 2.

ery after July 4th, 1857. The election took place in January, at which Charles Robinson was chosen Governor. Perhaps the most effective organization which carried the Kansas Free-State party through the most critical part of its existence was the Executive Committee, at whose head as chairman was Jas. H. Lane. It derived its existence from a primary convention held at Topeka September 19th.

GOVERNORS WOODSON AND SHANNON.—After the removal of Governor Reeder, July 28, 1855, Daniel Woodson was *acting* Governor of Kansas during the remainder of the session of the Territorial Legislature. Honorable Wilson Shannon, having accepted a commission as Governor of Kansas Territory, arrived at Shawnee September 3d. "He affirmed the legality of the Pawnee Legislature, and avowed himself as in favor of *slavery in Kansas.*"

"BEECHER'S BIBLES."—After the signal victory in the Territorial election the Pro-Slavery party became more and more intolerant and aggressive. An appeal for arms was made by the citizens of Lawrence. In May, 1855, cases marked "books" were received, containing 100 Sharps rifles, nicknamed "Beecher's Bibles." Henry Ward Beecher had said that these were the essential requisites for converting the pro-slavery element in Kansas.

Dr. Robinson, speaking of the first installment of arms, ("The Kansas Conflict," p. 124,) says: "These were indispensable. As soon as their arrival was known a change in the atmosphere was perceptible, most agreeable to the Free-State men and most chilling to the ardor of the Slave-State men."

THE CLIMAX REACHED.— Many were the deeds of lawlessness and murder, which the scope of this work will not permit us even to mention. Mr. William Phillips, of Leavenworth, signed a protest against the election of March 30th, in that city. Upon his refusal to leave the Territory as he was commanded, he was, on the 17th of May, 1855, seized by pro-slavery men, tarred and feathered, and sold at a mock auction for a dollar. He was subsequently murdered at his own house, by a company of " law-and-order " men.

The first man killed in Kansas Territory was a pro-slavery man. His slayer successfully plead self-defense. The second, also a violent pro-slavery man, Malcolm Clark by name, was killed at Leavenworth by Colonel McCrea. While the election was in progress at Leavenworth, a band of border-ruffians crushed in the windows where votes were being received, causing a panic among the officials. At Easton, another polling-place, Capt. R. P. Brown and his men had a skirmish with the opposition, in which one pro-slavery man was killed. Brown was soon after taken prisoner, and foully murdered with a hatchet. Rev. Pardee Butler, a fearless, outspoken free-soil man, was mobbed, tarred and feathered at Atchison, and then set adrift down the Missouri river on a small raft. On the 21st day of November, 1855, a pro-slavery man, F. N. Coleman, murdered Charles Dow, a Free-State man, at Hickory Point, Douglas county, some ten miles south of Lawrence. Dow was entirely unarmed. This was the immediate cause that brought about the " Wakarusa war."

CHAPTER IV.

RESCUE OF BRANSON.—Harrison Buckley, connected with
the murder of Dow, swore out a peace warrant against Ja-
cob Branson, at whose house Dow was accustomed to make
his home; he (Branson) having threatened to shoot Buckley at sight. The warrant was placed in the hands of the
postmaster of Westport, Missouri—Samuel J. Jones, recently commissioned sheriff of Douglas county, of whom
we shall learn much in succeeding pages. Jones, with his
posse of fifteen men, dragged Branson from his bed and
ordered him to mount a mule. While passing the house
of Mr. J. B. Abbott they were halted by Captain S. N.
Wood's company of fifteen Free-State men, and under
guns of both parties at a "ready, take aim," Branson rode
over to his friends.

Wood, as Branson's lawyer, asked Jones to produce his
warrant. This he could not or would not do, and after
an exchange of a storm of words Jones and his men proceeded on their way toward Franklin, minus their prisoner.

RAID ON LAWRENCE.—Jones, chagrined at his failure,
but secretly rejoicing that an excuse was given him to
strike his enemy a telling blow, hastily sent to his friends
in Missouri for help, and at the same time runners were
dispatched with exaggerated stories, to Gov. Shannon.
Kansas militia responded but feebly, while from the pro-
slavery towns, and Missouri, a motley crowd of 1500, heav-

(32)

ily armed with all manner of destructive implements, wended their way towards Lawrence, encamping on the Wakarusa, a small tributary of the Kaw, flowing south of the city. Shannon had sent to Leavenworth for troops. In the meantime in Lawrence all was military stir and bustle. What with the welcoming of companies of Free-State men from the surrounding country, rejoicing over several opportune consignments of Sharps rifles, fortifying for defense, and the continuous drill which the men were undergoing; no thought of surrender was entertained. Is it to be wondered that when rumor reached the town that they would be compelled to surrender their Sharps rifles, the significant remark was elicited, that they would "surrender their contents"?

Robinson and Lane were placed in command. The leaders counseled caution and moderation. That as the citizens of Lawrence had committed no untoward act, nothing should be done now that would give a coloring to the pro-slavery report, and to the proclamation of Governor Shannon, that the citizens of Lawrence were in open rebellion.

On the contrary, the committee sent a message to the Governor calling his attention to the presence of an armed force from a foreign State, who were committing depredations on the citizens, and asking whether it was by his order, and requesting their immediate removal. This message was conveyed through the enemy's lines, and was a dangerous undertaking. The names of the messengers were G. P. Lowry and C. W. Babcock.

The Governor concluded to personally investigate the condition of affairs, both at the pro-slavery camp and the city of Lawrence. Having done so, he impressed the pro-slavery gang that it would be utterly impossible for them to successfully attack Lawrence in its present fortified condition. On December 7th, Shannon visited Lawrence with several Missouri leaders, where, with the Free-State leaders, a treaty was agreed upon. Shannon disbanded the baffled Missourians, and Lawrence realized she had gained a victory — not by blood, but through strategy.

THE MURDER OF BARBER.— The only casualty on the part of the Free-State men, was the murder of Barber.* On the morning of the 6th of December, while riding unarmed toward his home with a brother and one other companion, Barber was shot by two pro-slavery men named Clarke and Burns. Because of Barber's peaceable and quiet disposition, and the unprovoked manner in which he was killed, there was great excitement among the soldiers gathered at Lawrence, and it was with difficulty that they were restrained from immediate and sanguinary retaliation. The army from Missouri took three dead bodies with them — two killed accidentally and one in some sort of a quarrel.

RESULTS OF THE WAKARUSA WAR.— The winter of 1855–56 in Kansas was very severe. The settlers in their unfinished log huts, especially the women and children, suffered untold hardships. But little of a war-like nature was done by the free-soilers, though preparations along the border indicated a more formidable invasion than had before been known. Six men were dispatched to the East for assistance. They hit upon the novel plan of secreting their credentials in jugs with corn-cob corks, while passing through Kansas and Missouri. They were successful in procuring material assistance for their Kansas brethren.

---

* "The Burial of Barber," Part 3.

The people of the South in the meantime were not idle. In Washington, Kansas principally occupied the attention of Congress. Plans, suggestions, bills and substitutes were numerous. But one, however, came to maturity. This provided for a committee of three who were sent to Kansas to investigate. A mass of evidence was procured, which was of no credit to either party in Kansas.

CHAPTER V.

PRO-SLAVERY AND FREE-STATE DEPREDATIONS.

JONES WOUNDED.—In the spring Jones became again active in his efforts to stir anew the strife, making several trips to Lawrence to arrest parties who had resisted or showed contempt for his authority. While in Lawrence on one of these unwelcome visits, he was shot and wounded by a reckless young man, J. P. Filer. This resulted again in great excitement among the pro-slavery men in Kansas and Missouri. "Down with the abolition town of Lawrence!" was the cry, "no matter what the cost or result."

TERRITORIAL INDICTMENTS.—In May the grand jury of Douglas county was in session, and under the instructions of Judge Lecompte, indictments for treason were found against Robinson, Lane, Reeder, and several others. Bills were also found against the two Free-State papers, the *Herald of Freedom* and *Kansas Free-State*, and against the "Free-State Hotel," which was "regularly parapeted and port-holed for the use of cannon and small arms." Reeder escaped in disguise down the Missouri river, thus saving his life. Robinson was arrested at Lexington, Missouri, while on his way east for assistance. Lane, by various strategic movements, avoided arrest.

SECOND RAID ON LAWRENCE.—United States Marshal Donaldson called upon citizens to rally at Lecompton. "Lawrence must be wiped from the face of the earth this time at all events." Missouri and border towns of Kansas responded. A peculiar assemblage threatened Lawrence. This town again resorted to a committee of safety, and, as formerly, assumed a non-combative attitude. Supplicatory messages were sent to Lecompton, but all to no purpose.

On the 19th of May, a young man named Jones, returning home from Lawrence, was halted near Blanton's bridge, disarmed, robbed, and murdered. Three boys who went out to investigate the affair returned in a few hours with their companion, Stewart, a corpse.

On the 21st, Deputy Marshal Fain rode into Lawrence with his posse and made arrests, no resistance being offered. The cannon was dug up and surrendered to Jones; also a few muskets. The Sharps rifles in the hands of a few individuals were refused. Jones and his gang then proceeded to demolish the two printing-presses and the obnoxious Free-State Hotel. Robberies and other indignities were indulged in, and as a finale the private dwelling of Robinson, on Mount Oread, was burned.

"Lawrence had not been conquered, for she had not resisted; but it proved the beginning of aggressive warfare on the part of the Free-State settlers, who up to this time, while boldly denying the validity or binding force of the Territorial law, had studiously avoided open conflict with the authorities by passively ignoring them." [*Andreas, p. 131.*]

When it was decided to offer no resistance, armed citizens disappeared from town, and those who remained were counseled to ignore the presence of marshals, sheriff, and posse, and as usual to proceed with their daily vocations.

OTHER DEPREDATIONS.—Straggling parties of pro-slavery men remained at Lecompton, and a party under Captain Pate and Coleman, the murderer of Dow, remained in the valley of the Wakarusa, threatening and robbing the settlers. This force was twice attacked by unknown parties, much to the discredit of the former.

FREE-STATE MEN RETALIATE.—"It was evident that reprisals were being made on the pro-slavery men. . . . In three days after the great 'law-and-order' victory at Lawrence, the whole surrounding country seemed to be infested with Free-State guerillas, who robbed and plundered the pro-slavery settlers, and harassed the 'law-and-order' troops without mercy. Shannon waxed wroth, and patrolled the country with his friend Col. Titus and members of his command. He now proved his utter incompetency to govern the people." It was while Donaldson and Jones were surrounding Lawrence, that Charles Sumner was delivering in Congress his famous speech, "The Crime Against Kansas," for which, while writing at his desk on the 22d of May, he fell under the brutal blows of Brooks of South Carolina.

CHAPTER VI.

MORE FIGHTING.

THE POTTAWATOMIE MASSACRE.—On the night of May 24th, 1856, six men under the leadership of John Brown, of Osawatomie, visited the valley of the Pottawátomie, and executed James Doyle, and his two sons, together with Allen Wilkerson and William Sherman. Historians are divided as to the occasion or result of this midnight foray; some claiming that it came near jeopardizing the Free-State cause in Kansas, in that it roused the opposition and their friends to a pitch bordering on frenzy. Others insist, with Brown, that a blow quick and dreadful was essential to stop the depredations that were being perpetrated by the Pro-Slavery party, and that it was the means of saving many lives and homes to the Free-State cause. It was one of the many incidents of border warfare which we fain would forget; failing in which, we pass it by with a shudder.

BATTLE OF BLACK JACK.—Captain H. C. Pate, who was still in the vicinity of Franklin, hearing of the Pottawatomie massacre, hastened to retaliate. A squad of his men attacked and plundered Palmyra, taking two prisoners. On June 1st, six pro-slavery men attacked Prairie City, while the people were at church. They were suddenly repulsed, however, with the loss of one man taken prisoner. Old John Brown, with twenty-eight men, attacked Pate at Black Jack, where his forces were encamped, protected by wagons in front and a ravine in the rear. After three hours' firing, Pate surrendered his remaining force of twenty-three men and quite an amount of army supplies. These were conveyed to Brown's camp. This timely attack and capture of Pate somewhat disconcerted the plans of Whitfield, Territorial Delegate to Congress, who, with an army collected from border towns, was pushing forward to join Pate, in conjunction with whom every Free-State man was to have been driven from the country.

DISPERSING THE INVADERS.— In the meantime, 150 Free-State men had congregated near Palmyra. Governor Shannon ordered all illegal armed bodies to disperse. Colonel Sumner, of the U. S. dragoons, appeared before John Brown's camp and ordered the prisoners released. John Brown reluctantly complied. About two miles from Brown's camp Sumner encountered a pro-slavery force of three hundred under Whitfield and General Coffey, of the militia. Sumner read to them the Governor's proclamation. The Missourians returned toward the border, killing several Free-State men on their way, and, sweeping southward, plundered the hated town of Osawatomie. It was only the fear of United States troops, and that Free-State men were near, that caused them to postpone the final settlement with this "abolition" home of John Brown.

KANSAS AID SOCIETY.— Because of these scenes recently enacted in Kansas, the excitement throughout the North became intense. The peaceful organization known as the Emigrant Aid Society, whose efforts were to locate and assist the true settler, was overshadowed by Kansas aid societies, whose object was to furnish men with arms to aid these settlers. Great meetings were held in all the large cities, and were addressed by Lane, Reeder, Wood, and Pomeroy. Large volunteer forces responded.

AGITATION IN THE SOUTH. — The Pro-Slavery party became frightened at the prospective current of abolition immigration. Fiery speeches of "southrons" produced large returns in men, money, and arms. A system of brigandage was adopted; all boats on the Missouri were inspected, and landings were patrolled by armed desperadoes denominated the "Law-and-Order" party, headed by Atchison of Missouri, Buford of South Carolina, and B. F. Stringfellow of Weston, Missouri, till it finally amounted to an absolute blockade. The Free-State men were eventually compelled to open another route, via Iowa and Nebraska, being the only way by which people from the north could enter Kansas Territory. Over this route came 500 immigrants under Lane, who crossed into Kansas from Nebraska on August 7th. Redpath followed in September with 130 men. Following on his heels came Eldridge and Pomeroy, of Lawrence, with 223 men well armed with rifles; Robert Morrow having been permitted to take these guns from the State arsenal of Iowa.

BATTLE OF FRANKLIN. — The Pro-Slavery party had erected various block-houses or forts, for the purpose of operating against Lawrence — one at Franklin; one at Washington creek, called Ft. Saunders; another near Lecompton, Ft. Titus. In June the fort at Franklin experienced a night attack, in which one of the defenders was killed and several wounded.

SECOND BATTLE OF FRANKLIN. — Again in August a party of 81 Free-State men under Lane attacked the fort. After discharging volley after volley for three hours, without dislodging the men in the fort, a wagon was filled with hay and drawn near the building and set on fire. A cry for quarter was raised from within — firing ceased — and the fort surrendered. A cannon was captured and taken to Lawrence and hidden in a cellar. A pattern of a ball was taken, and the type of the *Herald of Freedom*, destroyed by Jones and his posse, was moulded into bullets and hurled against the walls of Ft. Titus.

FORT SAUNDERS CAPTURED.—Meanwhile, the Franklin party had been reinforced by Captain Samuel Walker's men from Wakarusa valley, and 30 of the Chicago Rifles, from Topeka. The force, 400 strong, and "straw men" arranged in wagons, to augment the appearance of the force, proceeded to attack the fort on the afternoon of the 15th. The enemy seeing such a formidable force evacuated, leaving forty guns and a horse which belonged to a murdered man, D. S. Hoyt. This murder was the immediate cause of the attack on the fort. Lane with a few companions now returned to Nebraska, the command devolving on Capt. Walker.

FORT TITUS.*—The Free-State men, thinking the prisoners at Lecompton in danger of being murdered, started on a secret expedition for that place, but chanced to meet a company of Col. Titus's men. A skirmish took place, which destroyed the prospects of secretly rescuing the prisoners at Lecompton. Titus retreated to the fort. The cavalry, arriving first, made a charge, losing one man and had several wounded. The foot soldiers having now arrived with the cannon, "a new issue of the *Herald of Freedom*" was hurled against the sides of the fort. After thirty-six pounds of this type—"as set up by Captain Bickerton"—had been utilized, Col. Titus, wounded, and covered with blood, with his seventeen followers, surrendered. The pro-slavery loss was two killed and two wounded.

---

* "How we took Titus," Part 2.

The Free-State men lost Captain Shombré, killed, and six men wounded.

TREATY OF PEACE. — On the 17th, Governor Shannon, Major Sedgwick, and the postmaster at Lecompton, appeared in Lawrence to negotiate a treaty. The cannon taken by Jones at Lawrence, May 21st, was returned, and six prisoners charged with taking part in the attack on Franklin were released. In return, the Free-State men surrendered Titus and his men.

GOVERNOR SHANNON RESIGNS. — On the 28th of August Shannon wrote President Pierce: "I am unwilling to perform the duties of Governor of this Territory any longer. You will therefore consider my official connection with this Territory at an end." Toward the close of his administration, he, like Reeder, had incurred the enmity of the Pro-Slavery party, and was compelled to leave the Territory in fear of being murdered.

BATTLE OF OSAWATOMIE. — Secretary Woodson again became acting Governor. No check being placed upon the armed hordes of Missouri, they once more poured into Kansas. A party of 250 men under John W. Reid — a part of Atchison's army then encamped on Bull creek, fifteen miles north of Osawatomie — under the guidance of Martin White, appeared before Osawatomie at dawn, on the morning of August 30th. On the outskirts of the village they met Frederick, the son of Old John Brown, who was shot dead by this pro-slavery minister.

The leaders of the Free-State men, Capt. John Brown, Dr. W. W. Updegraff, and Captain Cline, were notified. Brown formed his little army of defenders south of the Marais des Cygnes. After firing several volleys, a cannon was brought to bear on the underbrush in which the Free-

State men were concealed. This failing to dislodge them, a general charge was ordered by Reid. Brown and his brave defenders were forced to retreat "on the plan of every man for himself." The town was burned and plundered; twelve covered wagons being used to carry off the booty and the wounded. Six Free-State men were killed. The pro-slavery loss was perhaps less than that number.

JOHN BROWN'S MONUMENT.—In the suburbs of the historic town of Osawatomie stands a plain marble shaft, on which are the following brief but impressive inscriptions:

"David R. Garrison, Geo. W. Partridge, Frederick K. Brown. In commemoration of those who fell on the 30th of August, 1856."

"This inscription is also in commemoration of Captain John Brown, who commanded at the battle of Osawatomie, August 30th, 1856.

"Who died and conquered American slavery on the scaffold, at Charlestown, Virginia."

On the other side of the monument are also found the names — "Theon Parker Powers.
                    Charley Keiser."

To the shame of the citizens of Osawatonie be it said, this monument is not inclosed, and vandals have been permitted to chip off the corners as souvenirs, and to write upon and otherwise deface the memento.

SEQUEL TO THE BATTLE OF OSAWATOMIE.— General Lane, having suddenly returned from Nebraska, hastily gathered a force of 300, principally from Topeka and Lawrence, and proceeded against Atchison, on Bull creek. Nothing came of the expedition. The hostile parties approached each other, exchanged a few scattering shots, and retired, Atchison toward Missouri and Lane toward Lawrence.

JOHN BROWN'S MONUMENT AT OSAWATOMIE.

MOVEMENT AGAINST LECOMPTON.—Depredations by pro-slavery men caused Lane to advance upon that town in two formidable columns. One under Colonel Harvey marched up the north side of the Kaw and got in position to cut off any retreat; but the troops under Lane, 300 strong, were from some cause delayed, and did not reach Lecompton till the following day, September 5th. In the meantime Colonel Harvey and his force returned toward Lawrence.

When Lane's men appeared before Lecompton all was consternation and confusion. A messenger was sent to the camp of Colonel Cooke, of the United States cavalry, with word that the city was about to be bombarded by a force 1,000 strong. Cooke appeared upon the scene, a parley ensued, the Free-State prisoners were sent over to their friends, and all returned to Lawrence the next day. These prisoners were not Robinson, Jenkins, and others, who were held by United States troops near Lecompton, awaiting trial for high treason.

RELEASE OF THE FREE-STATE PRISONERS.—The last oc-currence in Woodson's administration, worthy of note, was the liberation on bail of Governor Robinson and other Free-State men. They were never tried for treason. Later, Governor Robinson was arraigned on a charge of usurpation of office. The jury decided there could be no usurpation of office that did not exist.

CHAPTER VII.

GEARY's PLANS.—John W. Geary, of Pennsylvania, the newly-appointed Governor, reached Lecompton September 10th, 1856. The national administration realized that something must be done to quiet the disorders in Kansas. Governor Geary was expected to perform this task. His plan was to rise above party prejudice and treat all alike; to require that the laws be obeyed; to disband the militia and all other unauthorized bodies of armed men — relying on actual residents of the Territory in case an army was needed. On the 11th he issued his famous address and two proclamations — one disbanding armed forces then in the Territory, the other providing for the legal organization of the Territorial militia.

BATTLE OF HICKORY POINT.—The Governor's proclamation did not have the immediate effect anticipated. Lane decided at once to leave the Territory. He and thirty of his followers were near Osawkie on their way to Nebraska, when rumors of the burning of Grasshopper Falls and other pro-slavery depredations caused him to attempt to chastise them. He accordingly sent to Topeka for help. Captain Whipple responded with fifty men. On the 13th they marched against Hickory Point, Jefferson county, but finding it so well fortified decided it useless to attempt to dislodge the enemy without cannon, and sent to Lawrence for reinforcements and cannon. Meantime, Lane, hearing

(46)

of Geary's proclamation, dismissed Whipple's force, and proceeded on his way to Nebraska. Harvey marched directly across the country, and though unsupported, attacked the town, and after several hours fighting captured the whole pro-slavery force. The prisoners were released on parole and the victors started toward Lawrence. On the way they were captured by United States troops, Colonel Harvey making his escape. Several months of captivity ensued. Many were acquitted, while some were sentenced on March 2d, according to Gihon, to a term of from five to seven years in the penitentiary.

THIRD ATTEMPT TO DESTROY LAWRENCE. — In spite of inaugurals and proclamations, a large pro-slavery party pushed toward Lawrence by way of Franklin. The Governor, responding to the appeals of Free-State men, appeared at Lawrence on the 13th of September in company with Col. Cooke and three hundred cavalry. "The scare was premature," says Prof. Spring, "as the Missourians drew off under cover of darkness without pressing an attack." Governor Geary made a reassuring speech, and returned to Lecompton. On the 14th scouts arrived with the startling intelligence that a large force of the enemy were advancing. Affairs in Lawrence were indeed gloomy. Lane had disappeared. Col. Harvey and Captain Bickerton with the artillery were absent. Provisions and ammunition were scarce ; a force of three hundred poorly-armed men was all that could be mustered. Here and there "Old John Brown urged his favorite maxim, 'Keep cool and fire low.'" "He held no command, but did all in his power, advising, and by his words of counsel, inspiring the little squads that he visited at their various posts, with something of his own iron determination and contempt of danger." Two detachments were sent forward to check the enemy's advance; a running fire was continued for some time, after which the Missourians returned to camp for the night. The repulsing party lay on their arms watching against surprise, at the time of Governor Geary's arrival. The gray light of the morning showed to the anxious watchers the stars and stripes flaunting from Mt. Oread, cannon were frowning from its heights, and the white tents of Cooke's squadrons dotted its summit. The danger was over — Lawrence was saved!

FIRST THANKSGIVING IN KANSAS.— Governor Geary now found leisure to make a tour of observation through the Territory, and, after congratulating himself and the people on the peaceful condition of the country, appointed November 20th, 1856, "as a day of general praise and thanksgiving to Almighty God"— the first proclamation of the kind issued in Kansas Territory.

THE TOPEKA LEGISLATURE.— On January 6th, 1857, a few members of what was known as the "Topeka Legislature" met. Governor Robinson being absent and no quorum present, the minority adjourned to the following day. At the instance and connivance of Sheriff Jones and Judge Cato, several of the most prominent members were arrested. The remainder took a recess to June 9th. The arrested members were released on giving bail in the sum of five hundred dollars each. They were never afterward brought to trial.

THE TERRITORIAL LEGISLATURE.—This body met on the 12th day of January, 1857, and from beginning to end was bitterly opposed to Geary and his policy. The climax was reached when the notorious W. T. Sherrard—would-be successor to Sheriff Jones—was killed in a quarrel at Lecompton. Sherrard had previously insulted the Governor and threatened his life. The Legislature had espoused the cause of Sherrard. His timely death without doubt saved the life of the Governor. Governor Geary, becoming tired of the thankless task of trying, conscientiously, to perform his duties, resigned, and, like his predecessors, fled from the Territory.

CHAPTER VIII.

A CHAPTER IN POLITICS.

ACTING GOVERNORS WOODSON AND STANTON.—Secretary Woodson served again as acting Governor, from April 16th to May 27th. Though he did his best to stir up new strife, owing to his brief control of public affairs his rule was comparatively without incident. It was now apparent that Kansas could not be made a slave State, but leading men of the Pro-Slavery party thought that it might be made a Democratic State. Therefore the appointment of Robert J. Walker as Governor indicated a change in Federal tactics, viz.: that the work of a constitutional convention should be submitted to the people for their ratification or rejection. Meanwhile, Frederick P. Stanton had preceded the newly-appointed Governor to Kansas. He issued an address in which the policy of the new administration was outlined. Stanton caused a census to be taken, with a view to apportioning delegates to a constitutional convention. Owing to the fact that nineteen interior counties out of thirty-four in the State had no representation, the Free-State men ignored the election. As a result, the delegates to the Lecompton Convention were elected by a vote comprising less than one-fourth those shown by the census.

GOVERNOR WALKER.—May 26, 1857, Governor Walker reached the Territorial seat of government. He hoped to impress upon the people the fairness of his pacific and honorable policy, and that all controversies should be settled by the peaceful but decisive struggle of the ballot-box. The Topeka. Legislature, with a mass convention attached, convened June 9th. There were loud and wordy discussions, all of which concluded in the adoption of mild or unimportant measures.

At another convention of Free-State men, held at Topeka, July 15th, resolutions were passed favoring a participation in the fall elections, and calling a mass convention at Grasshopper Falls in August. August 26th, Free-State people met and reaffirmed their decision to take part in the election of Territorial officers.

THE ELECTIONS.—The 5th of October proved a harvest-time for Free-State men. Many fraudulent votes were polled; especially was this true in McGee and Johnson counties. Later in October, Walker threw out these returns on technical grounds. The Free-State party elected nine of the thirteen Councilmen and twenty-four of the thirty-nine Representatives. Thus Walker and Stanton fulfilled their public pledges that the polls should receive protection at their hands.

THE LECOMPTON CONVENTION.—The first convention of the Pro-Slavery party met at Lecompton, September 7th. After several days spent principally in organizing, this body adjourned to meet again October 19th. The motive for this delay was the election of members of the Legislature, the result of which would mark out largely the line of policy to be pursued. The convention after a lengthy debate extricated itself from the perplexing task of forcing a pro-slavery constitution upon a people largely anti-slavery, by submitting to the people only a part of the constitution. Ballots were to be prepared, "Constitution with slavery," or, "Constitution with no slavery."

The Free-State men thought this would utterly preclude all chance of success for them, as the slavery clause was so worded as to admit of slavery in Kansas whether they voted "for" or "against"; and further, "the vote as proposed must result in the acceptance of the constitution in some form, and the consequent repudiation of the Topeka Constitution and every Free-State movement made by the people of the Territory."

RESIGNATION OF WALKER AND REMOVAL OF STANTON.—At this juncture Governor Walker, becoming thoroughly disgusted with such nefarious proceedings, left the Territory and never returned. On December 17th he tendered his resignation. Acting Governor Stanton, at the urgent request of a majority of the members of the Legislature, in order to avert an immediate civil war, convened that body, for which act he was summarily removed.

FIRST FREE-STATE TERRITORIAL LEGISLATURE.—This Legislature convened, amid great rejoicing, at Lecompton, December 7th, 1857. The most important act passed was a provision for the submission of the Lecompton Constitution to a vote of the people on January 4th, 1858.

VOTE ON THE LECOMPTON CONSTITUTION, DECEMBER 21, 1857. The Free-State party took no part in this election, which resulted in an old-time one-sided fraudulent affair. The *bona fide* vote making Kansas a slave State was 3,121. The fraudulent votes cast were 3,012.

THE VOTE ON CONSTITUTION AND STATE OFFICERS.— According to previous arrangements by Free-State men, in convention, a ticket was nominated, and on January 4th,

1858, an election was held which was participated in by the entire Pro-Slavery party. Andreas estimated the votes at this time as follows. Total vote 17,000. Pro-Slavery votes 4,000; Free-State 13,000. Total population 55,000. The Free-State officers elected received majorities ranging from 301 to 696.. The vote on the Lecompton Constitution was almost unanimous against that instrument. The Free-State officers elected immediately prepared a memorial to Congress refusing to serve under the Constitution, and urging that body not to admit Kansas under it.

The Disposal of the Lecompton Constitution.— February 2d President Buchanan submitted the Lecompton Constitution to Congress, urging the immediate admission of Kansas as a State. March 22d the Constitution passed the Senate, but failed in the House. There a substitute was offered known as the "Crittenden-Montgomery Bill," which left the question to the people of Kansas. This substitute was rejected by the Senate, and the matter referred to a conference committee, which formulated the "English Bill." One provision was in the form of a bribe of large land grants to the new State, provided the Lecompton Constitution was adopted. "The proposition was simply an offer combining a bribe and a threat, tendered a free people in barter for their principles, and was met with the execration and repudiation it deserved." [*Andreas.*]

At an election held in Kansas August 2d, the English Bill and the Lecompton Constitution were disposed of as indicated by the following vote: For the proposition, 1,788; against the proposition, 11,300; majority against, 9,512.

Last of the Topeka Legislature.— On January 5th the

Topeka Legislature convened at Topeka. Governor Robinson in his message urged the importance of sustaining the Free-State organization, and without obstructing the course of events so long as the tendency was toward the establishing of the principles set forth in the Topeka Constitution.

When the 4th day of March arrived, the time set for the reassembling of the Legislature, no quorum appearing, it died a natural death. "The times had outgrown it, and it fell, not into disrepute, but disuse." "It had for three years been the shrine at which the whole Free-State party had worshipped, and the citadel of liberty that had never been surrendered to a foe. No truer, no braver band of freemen ever fought the desperate fight of freedom against such appalling odds as did those who defended it. Their names will go down the ages in imperishable renown as the unconquerable defenders of Free-State institutions under the ægis of the Topeka Free-State Constitution."

THIRD TERRITORIAL LEGISLATURE.—The third session of the Territorial Legislature commenced at Lecompton, January 4th, 1858, and on the 6th adjourned to Lawrence. Among the most important measures enacted were: The removal of the capital to Minneola (afterward declared illegal by the Attorney General), and a bill providing for the election of delegates to a constitutional convention to meet at Minneola. There was a question as to the legality of this bill, as it was passed after the legal term of the Legislature had closed.

MORE CONVENTIONS AND CONSTITUTIONS.—Notwithstanding the question of legality, the convention met at Minneola, organized, and adjourned to meet at Leavenworth

—hence the name "Leavenworth Constitution." But when a vote was taken on the adoption of the constitution only about 3,000 votes were cast for it out of a voting population of perhaps 15,000. "The stigma of its origin destroyed an otherwise excellent constitution."

Admission of Kansas to the Union was asked under this constitution. It was referred to the Committee on Territories, in which lethargic condition it still remains.

CHAPTER IX.

The reader must bear in mind that it is but an epitome of Kansas history which we attempt to record. Hence the earnest student is referred to the works of Andreas, Wilder, Spring, Robinson and others for a more extended discussion of the subject. While the foregoing sanguinary and political events were taking place, having direct connection with the history of the Territory, much desultory fighting was indulged in under the leadership of Captain James Montgomery and John Brown of the "Jayhawkers," and Captain Hamilton and G. W. Clarke of the Pro-Slavery party.

The southeast counties of Kansas, being off the line of Northern immigration, were for a long time the victims of pro-slavery aggression. Fort Scott seemed to be the pro-slavery stronghold.

BATTLE OF MIDDLE CREEK.—An evening in August, 1856, found Captain Davis's command from Fort Scott encamped on Middle creek, nine miles southwest of Osawatomie. Fate ordained that nearly an equal number of Free-State men under Captains Anderson, Cline, and Shore, should encamp in the same neighborhood. In the early morning an attack was ordered. The Free-State men, advancing rapidly, were fired on by the Missourians. The fire was returned at such a rate of interest that Captain Davis's command beat a hasty retreat, leaving several

(56)

prisoners and two wounded men, one of whom died, and a ready-cooked breakfast, not to mention a black flag inscribed with red letters, "Victory or death."

CAPTAIN CLARKE'S EXPLOITS.—In the fall of 1856, Geo. W. Clarke, who murdered Barber during the Wakarusa war, at the head of a band of Missourians undertook to intimidate and drive out Free-State settlers by burning buildings, destroying crops, and "taking anything he wanted," until a soldier of the Black Hawk war who had also fought in the wars of the United States was led to say, "I never saw anything so bad and mean in my life as I saw under General Clarke."

JAMES MONTGOMERY.*—Compelled to hide to save his life because of Clarke, and at first to fight his enemies single-handed, was one James Montgomery, who afterward developed into one of the most active and deadly enemies to the Pro-Slavery party. Montgomery, seeing no attempt at redress by law, at last formed a company of his neighbors and took the field—making strategic raids on the enemy whether in Missouri or Kansas. "This bold and decided course of the Free-State men had the desired effect, peace for the time being was secured, and Montgomery returned to his home."

MARAIS DES CYGNES.—Captain A. C. Hamilton was reported as having made a list of Free-State men who were to be "put out of the way." This list fell into the hands of the ever-vigilant Montgomery, who determined to kill Hamilton at the first opportunity. About May 1st, Montgomery with a party of men and a howitzer approached the log house of Hamilton, and, had it not been for the

---

* "James Montgomery," Part 2, (Moody's Poem.)

approach of United States troops, we doubtless should not have to chronicle the Marais des Cygnes massacre* as an event in Kansas history. The death list referred to was given by Captain Montgomery to the sheriff of Linn county, who assured Montgomery that the men who were proscribed would be protected. But justice, as usual in those days, lagged, and Hamilton unexpectedly made his appearance, arrested Patrick Ross, B. L. Reed, W. A. Stilwell, Asa and William Hairgrove, Austin and Amos Hall, William Colpetzer, W. Robertson, Asa Snyder, and John F. Campbell, (all quiet, inoffensive citizens,) took them to a ravine, drew them up in line, and deliberately shot them. Five were killed, five wounded, and one feigned death and fell with the others. The killed were Campbell, Colpetzer, Ross, Stilwell, and Robertson. Montgomery returned on the evening of the massacre. A pursuit was instituted, but nothing was done with Hamilton. Five years afterward one of his men, William Griffith, was tried, convicted, and afterward hanged by one of the wounded men, Asa Hairgrove.

JOHN BROWN AGAIN IN KANSAS.—In the fall of 1858 Old John Brown, who had been invited into Linn county by one Augustus Wattles, to assist in fighting the proslavery men, was introduced under the assumed name of Shubal Morgan, his personal safety and the success of his maneuvers requiring it. Brown's first aggressive movement was a raid into Missouri, where he liberated 17 slaves. December 20th, Brown's men in two detachments—one under Brown, the other under J. H. Kagi—paid their respects to Missouri the second time. Brown's party was successful in liberating ten slaves. Kagi's party liberated

---

* "Le Marais du Cygne," Part 2.

one slave and killed one white man. This caused so much excitement that the Governor of Missouri offered $3,000 for Brown's arrest, and President Buchanan offered $250 for his head. Brown took his negroes into Franklin county, where he secreted them for a month in an old cabin near Lane. He then moved north, and when near Holton a band of pro-slavery men from Atchison tried to recapture his negroes, but were compelled to beat a hasty retreat. This event is known as the "Battle of the Spurs."

JOHN BROWN'S FAMOUS PARALLELS.*—While in Franklin county, John Brown wrote his "Parallels," dating at Trading Post to shield himself and friends from suspicion, and that his plans might be successful.

---

* "John Brown's Parallels," Part 2.

CHAPTER X.

FIRST REPUBLICAN PARTY IN KANSAS.—The most notable political event of 1859, in Kansas, was the organization of the Republican party of Kansas, at Osawatomie, on the 18th of May. After the organization was completed, the great and good Horace Greeley addressed the convention.

GOVERNORS DENVER AND MEDARY. — On March 15, 1858, Secretary Denver became acting Governor of Kansas Territory, but did not take the oath of office till May 12th of that year. The following words of praise from his political opponent, Governor Robinson, speak volumes in praise of his administration: "It is enough to say of Secretary, and afterward Governor, Denver that he proved to be as goód as his word, and the Territory under his administration prospered politically as well as materially. In the disturbances of southern Kansas, and in every position, he acted with impartiality, and gained the confidence of the *bona fide* residents of the Territory, and of all parties." "This high praise, coming as it did from one of his leading political opponents, did not exceed the acknowledged deserts of the upright and faithful official upon whom it was bestowed." [*Andreas.*]

He was censured by the Pro-Slavery party for making a treaty with Captain Montgomery. He was compelled to resign, to forestall removal by the President.

The administration of the last of the Territorial governors,

Samuel Medary, was uneventful. To put an end to feuds that were still agitating different portions of the Territory, he issued a general amnesty proclamation to all who had committed crimes because of political disturbances in Kansas.

KANSAS FAMINE, 1860.—Excessive drought caused a failure of crops throughout the Territory. Later, myriads of grasshoppers in many places completed the destruction of growing vegetation. Springs and wells dried up. Scarcely a family escaped the ague, or malarial fever in some form, resulting frequently in death. The suffering was increased by the severe winter of 1860–61. Snow fell to a depth of two feet, remaining on the ground six weeks. The settlers felled trees, that the stock might subsist on the buds, or browse. Nothing but charity stood between many of the people and starvation. But through the liberality of the East, 8,090,951 pounds of provisions and 2,500 bushels of seed wheat were distributed at Atchison. Besides this, churches and individuals sent relief to friends in Kansas. So difficult was it to transport these goods to the interior because of the condition of the horses and oxen, that many who could do so freighted on shares, receiving half for their services. It is estimated that 30,000 settlers "went back to wife's folks" in 1860. Fortunately, the storms drove the buffalo further east than they had roamed for years, and though they were thin in flesh, they were gladly killed and eaten by the western settlers.

KANSAS ADMITTED.—In 1859 the Legislature passed an act authorizing yet another constitutional convention. On the 28th of March this proposition was submitted to the people—three-fourths of the votes being favorable. The election of delegates occurred June 7th, and on the 5th of July the convention met at Wyandotte and framed a constitution. In October it was ratified by the people; then followed the election of State officers on December 6th. Dr. Robinson was elected first Governor of the State. The bill admitting Kansas into the Union was signed by President Buchanan, January 29th, 1861, and Kansas became the thirty-fourth State of the Union.

How the News was Received.—In Kansas the news is received with great rejoicing and bonfires. The Leavenworth *Conservative* prints an extra, and D. R. Anthony carries it to Lawrence; Captain Swift and others dig up the historic gun "Old Sacramento," (buried near Clinton, in Douglas county,) go to Lawrence and help celebrate. Songs and speech-making were indulged in till nearly morning of the following day.

State Seal.—In 1861, Mr. Ingalls writes: "The vexed question of a State seal has at last received its quietus at the hands of a conference committee. The new design embraces a prairie landscape with buffalo pursued by Indian hunters, a settler's cabin, and a plowman with his team, a river with a steamboat, a cluster of thirty-four stars surrounding the legend, 'Ad Astra per Aspera,' the whole encircled by the words, 'Great Seal of the State of Kansas. 1861.'"

Origin of Name and Meaning of Motto.—The name Kansas is an Indian word, and means Smoky Water. Some, however, insist—and with a good show of reason—that the name signifies "Child of the Wind." The motto "Ad Astra per Aspera" is from the Latin, and means "To the stars through difficulties."

CHAPTER XI.

KANSAS DURING THE CIVIL WAR.

Within three months after being admitted to the Union, Kansas was called upon to furnish her quota of troops to defend that Union. From June, 1861, to July, 1864, Kansas raised seventeen regiments, 20,097 men — being 3,443 more than her quota, and more soldiers in proportion to population than any other State. Statistics show that the per cent. of killed, and deaths from disease, was greatest among Kansas troops.

LAWRENCE RAID, 1863.*—In the afternoon of August 20, Quantrill, a famous guerrilla chief, crossed the Missouri line into Kansas; marched rapidly and quietly throughout the night toward Lawrence; passed through the towns of Gardner and Hesper, reaching an eminence near the doomed city about sunrise, August 21st; here a parley was held, many declaring it would be madness to attack the town; Quantrill avowed he would enter the town alone. This bold assertion imbued the followers with some of the spirit of their leader. Two horsemen were sent through the town on a reconoissance, and returned with the gratifying report that the town was asleep. A wild charge was made upon the town by the 175 raiders. They dashed through the main streets shouting like demons, and shooting right and left at people on the sidewalks or at the windows. After getting possession

* Read "Lawrence Raid," by Ellen Patton, Part 2, and "A Border Memory," Part 2.

of the Eldridge House, (formerly Free-State Hotel,) from which they had expected resistance, they scattered throughout all parts of the town burning and plundering buildings and murdering inhabitants.

Promises to save the town, if no resistance was offered, induced many to surrender, who were immediately murdered. "Burn every house and kill every man," was the leader's command. "It is doubtful if the world ever witnessed such a scene of horror," writes one. "As the scene at their entrance was one of the wildest, the scene after their departure was one of the saddest that ever met mortal gaze." On one street 75 buildings were destroyed. The streets and walks were lined with dead bodies, many being charred so that they could not be recognized. The whole number killed was 143 and twenty-five wounded. Nearly two millions of dollars' worth of property was stolen or destroyed.

About the middle of the forenoon the raiders, freshly mounted, and loaded with booty, started for Missouri.

Lane collected about 35 followers and gave chase. Though this company and 250 men under Major Plumb came up with the raiders, for some reason the blow was not struck, and the ruffian band escaped.

PRICE RAID.—In October, 1864, General Sterling Price attempted to invade Kansas. Troops under Generals Curtis and Blunt, in western Kansas fighting Indians, were called to repel the invasion. The Governor of Kansas issued a proclamation calling out the entire State militia, amounting to 12,622 men.

BATTLE OF LEXINGTON. — The troops under Blunt and Lane, though outnumbered ten to one, made desperate attempts to check Price's advance, fighting continually for eight hours while retreating from Lexington toward Independence. The Union loss was 200. The enemy's loss was reported at 500.

BATTLE OF THE BIG BLUE.—On the morning of the 22d Curtis's army took position along the banks of the Big Blue. Colonel Jennison held his position at Byrom's ford by raking the enemy with his howitzers, till the rebels flanked him by utilizing cattle fords; he then retreated toward Westport. Here he was reinforced by Colonel Moonlight, Major Hunt, and others. A movement was made against Shelby's advance, and he was forced back to the Big Blue, where he encamped that night. While this repulse was taking place, the Shawnee County Militia under Colonel Veale were compelled to fight six times their number, in which battle they lost over 100 men in killed, wounded, and missing.

BATTLE OF WESTPORT.—On the 22d, the army at Westport was reinforced by General Pleasonton with 7,000 cavalry and several pieces of artillery.

Early in the morning of the 23d the advancing Union forces met the enemy, and after a sharp contest of varying fortunes the enemy were driven into an open prairie and a precipitate retreat ensued.

PURSUIT OF PRICE.—Price's retreat was along the State line, southwesterly to Linn county, thence in the direction of Fort Scott, then eastward through Missouri to the south of the Arkansas river. He was hotly pursued by Kansas troops, who continually harassed his flanks and rear, and bringing him to engagements at Trading Post and Mine Creek, in Linn county, Kansas. At the latter place they captured Major General Marmaduke, three brigadiers, and 800 men.   Another sharp-conflict took place at Osage crossing, in Kansas.   On the 29th a general engagement took place at Newtonia, Missouri.   Price fled along the Cassville road.

CHAPTER XII.

INDIAN WARS.

In April, 1864, there was a general uprising of the Indians of the plains, and for months a cruel war was waged against the settlers of Kansas. War was kept up almost continually for six years. Alarms and attacks on some defenseless settlement were of frequent occurrence. After one of these Indian raids the settlers would, if possible, organize and pursue the savages, who usually, however, made good their escape.

An army of militia under Curtis, in pursuit of Indians, was recalled to suppress the Price raid in 1864.

PAWNEES AND OMAHAS.—During 1865 and 1866, Pawnees and Omahas attacked and murdered many settlers in the northwestern part of Kansas.

In April, 1867, United States troops under General Hancock totally destroyed an Indian village of 300 lodges, on Pawnee Fork. The Indians, by way of retaliation, assailed the whole Kansas frontier. Travel on the overland routes through Kansas to New Mexico and Colorado was almost entirely stopped.

WAR WITH THE CHEYENNES, ARAPAHOES, AND KIOWAS.—In June these tribes attacked the frontier of Kansas, and the engineering parties on the Kansas Pacific Railroad in the western part of the State. Eight companies of Kansas volunteer cavalry were organized, and proceeded against the Indians. August 21st, a portion of the Tenth cavalry was attacked by a large force of Indians on the Republican river. After hard fighting by this little force of 150, they were forced to retreat. The Indian loss was 150. The whites lost three killed and 35 wounded. The Eighteenth and Seventh Kansas cavalry engaged in battle with the same Indians, signally defeating them.

RAID OF 1868.—Notwithstanding a treaty of peace made in October, 1867, the Cheyennes and Arapahoes 400 strong, after being armed by the Government, attacked the frontier settlements of southwest Kansas early in the spring, raiding the country as far east as Council Grove.

At about the same time a large party of Cheyennes raided all that country between the Saline and Republican — 60 miles in width — killing and scalping 40 whites.

In September, 1868, Governor Crawford caused five companies of militia to be organized, which patrolled the frontier from Nebraska to Wichita, doing much efficient service amid great hardships.

GENERAL SULLEY'S CAMPAIGN.—In September, General Sulley, with nine companies of cavalry, went to the south of the Arkansas, made war on the families and stock of the Indians, in order to draw the war-parties from Kansas. On the 21st he met a war-party of Indians and killed 17 of their number.

NINETEENTH KANSAS CAVALRY.—This regiment of 1200 men, commanded by Governor Crawford in person, took the field in the Indian territory, but failed to bring the Indians to battle.

BATTLE OF THE WACHITA.—At midnight of the 27th of November, 1868, General Custer surprised and attacked the Indians on the Wachita river. The fighting lasted several hours; the Indians fighting from ravines and timber. Chiefs Black Kettle and White Rock with 101 warriors were killed. Fifty-one lodges, together with many horses and mules, were captured. Custer lost 21 killed and 14 wounded.

CLOSE OF THE WAR.—The Indians did not recover their defeat at Wachita, but fell back, and were finally forced to make a treaty entirely satisfactory to the whites.

These Indian wars cost Kansas more than a thousand lives, and a million dollars to individuals, retarding settlement for many years.

Incursions into southwestern Kansas continued from time to time till 1878, since which time the Indians have been comparatively at peace.

CHAPTER XIII.

IN MEMORIAM.

COLONEL JAMES MONTGOMERY.*—Colonel James Montgomery was born in Ohio, in 1814. He was a cousin of Richard Montgomery, who fell at the storming of Quebec. He received an excellent academic education. He migrated to Kentucky in 1837, where he taught school several years. He lived in Missouri one year, and then came to Kansas, locating in Linn county, about five miles west of Mound City. Like John Brown, he was a praying fighter, hence a dangerous enemy. He served as colonel during the civil war, at the close of which he returned to his farm in Linn county, where he died, and was buried December 6th, 1871.

JAMES H. LANE.—Born in Lawrenceburg, Ind., June 22, 1814. Little is known of his early life. He was restive, and not fond of books. He served as colonel of the Third Regiment Indiana Volunteers, and did good service, in the early campaign of General Taylor in the Mexican war. He subsequently became Lieutenant Governor of Indiana, and later a member of Congress from that State. In Kansas he became the acknowledged leader of the most radical faction of the Free-State men. When the State was admitted to the Union he was chosen Senator, in 1861. During the rebellion he took an active part in recruiting for the United States service. Because of his irregular

---

* Read "James Montgomery," Part 2, (Moody's Poem.)

methods in this work, he incurred the enmity of the Governors of Kansas. He was finally commissioned Brigadier General of volunters. In 1864–65 he was again elected to the United States Senate. He took sides with President Johnson in his contest with Congress. Upon his return to Kansas, finding his influence gone, he committed suicide, July 1, 1866 — living, however, till the 11th. His body was laid to rest at Lawrence, where a plain white shaft with the inscription "Lane" marks his resting-place. "His faults, which were many, may well find sepulture with his mouldering dust. His virtues are enshrined in the hearts of the thousands all over Kansas who still revere his memory as their great leader, counselor, and friend."

BIOGRAPHY OF JOHN BROWN.

John Brown, styled "Osawatomie," was born in Torrington, Conn., May 9, 1800, and was hanged at Charlestown, Va., (now West Virginia,) on December 2, 1859. He was fifth in descent from Peter Brown, who landed at Plymouth, Mass., from the Mayflower, Dec. 11, 1620. He received a strictly religious education, and at the age of 19 went to Plainfield, Mass., with the intention of entering the Calvinistic ministry, but an affection of the eyes compelled him to return to his father's home, at Hudson, Ohio, where he became a tanner, as was his father before him.

In 1840 he embarked in the wool trade, and six years afterward removed to Springfield, Mass., and opened a wool warehouse. He attempted to establish a system of wool grading, which drove his New England customers to buying direct from the producers in the West, whereupon he took a cargo of wool to London, sold it for half its value, and returned a ruined man.

In 1849 he removed to North Elba, Essex county, N. Y.,

where he attempted to found a negro colony, he having for years harbored the thought of becoming the liberator of the Southern slaves; but the inclement climate and stubborn soil were too much for the colonists, and the project was a failure.

In 1854 his four eldest sons migrated to Kansas and settled in Lykins county, about eight miles from the village of Osawatomie. As they were abolitionists they were presently harassed and plundered by the "border-ruffians" of that day, and to their support went John Brown with a store of arms and ammunition. Trained by a life of toil to endure hardships, tough and sinewy of body, strictly temperate in his habits, and a brave, resolute, and God-fearing man, he was singularly fitted to become a leader in the rough encounters which marked the border warfare of 1854–56.

After some desultory fighting which developed his powers of generalship, in the latter part of August, 1856, a body of 250 Missourians marched upon the town of Osawatomie, which was held by Brown with only thirty men, and there, by his vigorous defense and masterly tactics, he earned his sobriquet.

During the next two years he devoted his energies to training men for what he declared the inevitable appeal to arms to wipe out slavery. About 10 o'clock on the night of Sunday, October 16, 1859, he with three of his sons, 19 other whites and 5 negroes entered the village of Harper's Ferry, Va., where stood a United States arsenal containing between 100,000 and 200,000 stand of arms, which he intended for the use of the thousands of slaves whom he thought would hasten to join him. Brown took possession of the arsenal, which by nightfall of the next day was surrounded by Virginia militia, and, after fighting bravely, Brown with a remaining force of three whites and a few blacks, changed his quarters to an adjoining engine house. At 7 o'clock on the morning of October 18, this refuge was taken by storm, and Brown, fighting desperately to the last, was struck down by a sabre-stroke, and while prostrate on the ground was twice bayoneted.

On the 27th his trial for "conspiring with negroes to produce insurrection, for treason against the commonwealth of Virginia, and for murder," began; four days afterward he was condemned to be hanged. On the morning of his execution he left the jail "with a radiant countenance and the step of a conqueror," pausing for a moment by the door to kiss a negro child held up to him by its mother. He met his death with perfect composure and tranquility. His body was buried at North Elba, where Wendell Phillips pronounced the funeral oration. The whole country was alive with excitement, and the song "John Brown's body lies a-mouldering in the grave" served greatly to stir up the patriotism of the North when the gun fired at Sumter gave the signal for civil war.

CHAPTER XIV.

PEACE.

At the close of the civil war, Kansas experienced comparative peace. For twelve years bloody internecine strife had held sway. That which costs most is usually most highly prized. Is it any wonder that this people love Kansas, and that the combined energies of a people who knew not the word failure have placed Kansas in the front rank of the sisterhood of States? There are no thrilling events to chronicle during this era; but silent forces make largely the history of a commonwealth. No attempts will be made to record, in order, the development during its era of peace. We have only space for a brief mention of a few institutions in which the average Kansan takes special pride.

KANSAS STATE HISTORICAL SOCIETY.—Secretary F. G. Adams contributes the following interesting facts: "The Kansas State Historical Society was established in 1875, at the suggestion of the Kansas Editors and Publishers Association. At a meeting of that body in Manhattan, April 7, 1875, on motion of Hon. D. W. Wilder a resolution was adopted for the appointment of a committee to organize the Society, 'for the purpose of saving the present and past records of our twenty-one years of eventful history.' The committee was composed as follows: F. P. Baker, D. R. Anthony, John A. Martin, Sol. Miller, and George A. Crawford. The Society was organized the De-

(74)

cember following. Seventeen years of Kansas history has
been added to the twenty-one years named in the resolution passed by the editors. The collections of the Historical Society have been kept in the State House at Topeka
from the beginning. By law the Society has been made
the trustee of the State, and its library and collections are
the property of the State, for the free use of the people. In
the seventeen years of its work the Society has gathered a
library consisting, according to the report of 1891, of
12,950 volumes of bound books, 11,414 bound newspaper
files, and 40,152 unbound books and pamphlets, making
in all a library of 64,516 volumes. The books and pamphlets consist of all that have been published in Kansas,
including the documents of the State, the publications of
the State institutions, and books issued by private authors
and publishers. The publications of churches, schools, and
societies of every kind are brought into this library. Of
the newspaper volumes in the library 8,412 are of Kansas
newspapers. The Society has, during the seventeen years
of its existence, been receiving and binding up every issue
of every paper and periodical published in Kansas, with
very few exceptions.

"Reading libraries do not generally contain pamphlets,
but in a library of historical reference, pamphlets are
found invaluable. Almost all the reports of societies and
institutions are issued in pamphlet form. They contain
the exact details of the history of the work of the bodies
issuing them. Each shows what has been the work of
some band of thoughtful, zealous and progressive people
in organized effort, during the period covered by such report. The reports of charitable organizations, schools,
colleges, educational conventions, missionary associations,

scientific bodies, of persons engaged in scientific, social and economic studies, in labor organizations, and of people engaged in all the different social and business enterprises which mark the present active and progressive age. Very many of the more valuable publications of the U. S. Government and of the State governments are in pamphlet form. Many of these are of great value and show the result of original scientific research and of industrial experiments.

"The library contains many thousand pages of manuscript. Manuscripts of early missionaries, and persons connected with missionary affairs, and of narratives and reminiscences of the early Kansas pioneers. The galleries of the Society contain portraits of the early Governors, public men of Kansas and of many early pioneers, and hundreds of such portraits are contained in cases in the rooms of the Society. Hundreds of relics illustrative of history are contained in the collection."

STATE REFORM SCHOOL.*— This school is three miles north of Topeka, on 160 acres of land donated by Topeka and Shawnee county. The buildings consist of main building, two cottages, chapel, engine house, bakery, hospital, and green-house. It was opened on a small scale, June 6, 1882. In July, 1892, there were enrolled 220 boys. Incorrigibles are not admitted as formerly, but those only who have committed crime for which they are liable to imprisonment.

STATE INDUSTRIAL SCHOOL FOR GIRLS.— This institution is located at Beloit, Mitchell county. The building is a three-story stone structure, erected on eighty acres of land donated by the city of Beloit. It had its beginning

*Read "The State Reform School," Part 2.

under the auspices of the Woman's Christian Temperance Union, Feb. 1st, 1888. The need of State aid for the protection and training of wayward girls became evident, and the Legislature of 1889 appropriated funds for the erection of the present substantial building. The number of inmates for the fiscal year ending June 30, 1892, reached one hundred. The scope of the work in the school is designed to be three-fold, viz.: Physical, in the mastery of the details of housekeeping; mental, in acquiring an education that will assist the pupil in the ordinary vocations of life; and moral, by proper influences thrown about them during the impressionable portion of their lives. These girls soon acquire a pride in making the school a happy home, and in honoring their benefactor, the State of Kansas. This is one of the most interesting and praiseworthy institutions of the State.

STATE NORMAL SCHOOL.—This institution is situated at Emporia. The Legislature granted 34,400 acres of land, and the minimum price was fixed at five dollars per acre. The school opened in 1865, with eighteen pupils. The enrollment of 1891 was nearly 1,400. A diploma from this institution is a life certificate to teach in Kansas. Tuition is free. Railroad fare in excess of three dollars is refunded to all Kansas students. "In buildings, in equipment, in the ability of its faculty, in the enthusiasm of its students, in the thoroughness of its work, the school now stands recognized as one of the best in the West, and as most worthy the confidence and patronage of the good people throughout the State."

THE KANSAS STATE AGRICULTURAL COLLEGE was located at Manhattan, in 1863. The objects of the institution are outlined in the report of the Regents in 1873. "To impart a liberal education to those who desire to qualify themselves for the actual practice of agriculture, the mechanic trades, or industrial arts. Prominence shall be given to the several branches of learning which relate to agriculture and the mechanic arts according to the directness and value of the relation." Tuition is free. · Pupils are admitted on having passed an examination of a required standard. Encouragement is given to daily habits of · manual labor. during the college · course. Only one hour's practice is required per day, but students are encouraged to make use of the opportunities for àdding to their means and ability.

KANSAS STATE UNIVERSITY.—On the day that Kansas' was admitted into the Union, Congress donated 46,080 acres of land for a State University in Kansas. In 1863 the question came up in the Legislature as to the location of this desirable institution. The fact that Amos A. Lawrence had donated $10,000, with accrued interest, and that Lawrence proposed to give to the State forty acres of land for a building-site, decided the location in favor of Lawrence. The University of Kansas was the first State institution in the United States to adopt the plan of co-education of the sexes.

RAILROADS.—Kansas people commenced early to build railroads, the first rail having been laid in Doniphan county, opposite St. Joseph, Missouri, in March, 1860. Because of the large increase in agricultural products, and the rapid development of the mines of the West, Kansas is now gridironed with railroads. It is estimated that there are now (1892) nearly 9,000 miles of railroads in actual operation within the State.

GROWTH IN POPULATION AND WEALTH.—Through the

kindness of Secretary Mohler, we are enabled to give the following:

"Kansas possesses a wealth of resources in soil and climate which is destined to place her among the most wealthy and prosperous States of the Union. The growth in wealth and population is remarkable. In 1880 the total assessed valuation of real and personal property of the State, including railroads, was $160,570,761.43; in 1890 it was $347,717,218.42; increase in decade, $186,-146,457.39. The true value was about four times that, or $1,200,000,000. The population in 1880 was 996,096; in 1890, 1,427,096; being an increase of 431,000. The assessed valuation per capita in 1880 was $161.20; in 1890 it had increased to $243.70.

"*Agriculture.*—The agricultural wealth has also grown at a corresponding rate. In 1880 the area in field crops was 8,868,884 acres, and the value of farm products was $63,111,634. In 1891 the area in field crops was 17,518,-018 acres, and the value of farm products, $121,695,245. In 1890 the aggregate number of horses, mules, sheep and swine was 5,640,476, valued at $113,533,342. The product of live-stock animals slaughtered and sold for slaughter, etc., increased in value from $16,933,255 in 1880 to $39,-998,225 in 1890. As a wheat-producing State Kansas ranks first, her product this year (1892) being about seventy millions of bushels. As a corn-producing State she ranks fourth — Iowa, Missouri and Illinois surpassing her in the amount of corn grown. In the production of oats she also takes about fourth place.

"As a fruit-growing State Kansas has also come to the front. Her soil and climate in the eastern half of the State is especially adapted to the apple, pear, cherry, apricot, and for all kinds of small fruits; while in southern Kansas peaches are also grown quite successfully.

"The healthfulness of the climate, fertility of the soil, the character of the people for intelligence and sobriety, make Kansas one of the first States in the Union."

CHURCHES.—In 1890, Kansas had 3,803 church organizations, and 2,339 church edifices, with an aggregate value of church property amounting to $8,801,870.

PUBLIC SCHOOLS.—The records of the State Superintendent show that, as in everything else, Kansas has made phenomenal headway educationally. In 1860 the total amount raised for school purposes was $19,212. There were only 7,029 persons of school age. State Superintendent Goodnow, in a review of educational progress in 1863, said :

"To retard the course of education we had first the border troubles of 1855 and 1856 ; the financial crisis of 1857; the drouth of 1860; and lastly, the rebellion of 1861. If with one-seventh of our population in the army, with the excitement of guerrilla raids, we can show continual progress in the work of education, no higher compliment can be paid to the virtue, intelligence, and heroism of our citizens. Truly, we can thank God and take courage."

Kansas had in 1891, 11,188 schools; a school population of 497,022, with an enrollment of 389,570, and an attendance of 246,102. During the year 189 school-houses were built. With her 9,041 school buildings and 11,240 rooms, and an estimated value of school property aggregating $10,298,061, Kansas makes a showing of which her people may well be proud.

TEMPERANCE.—It has been said that "Kansas leads the

van for reform." In early Territorial days a law was enacted "To regulate the sale of intoxicating liquors." In November, 1880, a prohibitory amendment to the State Constitution was submitted to the people. The vote cast on the amendment was 176,606. The majority in favor of the amendment was 7,998. It is useless for anyone to deny the fact that the sentiment in favor of prohibition in Kansas has steadily increased, and that drunkenness and crime have been materially lessened. The teaching of temperance in the public schools is, by statute, made compulsory.

PART II.

A COLLECTION FROM KANSAS AUTHORS.

COLLECTIONS.

A KANSAS WISH.

May Kansas skies e'er shower on you
Golden gifts from their vaults of blue;
 May Kansas winds that ceaseless blow,
 Now fierce and high, now soft and low,
Bring with them in their course so free
Bright, fadeless crowns of praise for thee.

May thy sorrows vanish e'er scarce they're found,
 Like Kansas snow;
And leave no trace on life's background
 As they lightly go.

While thy joys shall cling with lingering hold,
 Like Kansas wealth;
And their mark remain in the letters bold
 Of springing health.

May the force of thy foes be quickly spent,
 Like Kansas storms;
And no harm to thee with its strength be blent,
 Whate'er its forms.

While thy friends stand faithful, firm and true,
 Like Kansas soil;

Nor quickly change for the old the new
    In life's turmoil.

- May the Kansas air thy heart imbue   .
    With a spirit pure as the Kansas dew ;
        May the boundless prairies stretching here,
        Now fresh and green, now brown and sere,
    So lift thy soul that there shall be
    A broader, larger life for thee.

Charles Moreau Harger.

A KANSAS COLLECTION.

For about four years the writer has been engaged in the collection of a Kansas library. A shelf was at first set apart for the reception of Kansas books. The shelf overflowed and became two. The two have now become a reasonably filled alcove. As these books have gradually increased in number, enthusiasm for all that pertains to Kansas has correspondingly increased. They have been a constant source of pleasure, and a pure spirit of charity would prompt him to enter upon a crusade in favor of a Kansas shelf in every Kansas library.

The reasons why every Kansan should have a collection of Kansas books are many.

1. We cannot have an adequate knowledge of what Kansas is, and especially has been, unless we know something of her books.

Take for instance that heroic period from '55 to '58, when the prelude to the war was being fought on Kansas soil. We are now a third of a century from those times. Speak of John Brown, John Doy, Judge Lecompte, Sheriff Jones, Benjamin F. Stringfellow, Senator Atchison, Charles Robinson, James H. Lane, James Redpath, A. D. Richardson, Richard J. Hinton, Governors Geary, Reeder, the murder of Barber, the raids on Lawrence, the wild propensities of the Missourians to vote, the Pottawatomie murders—the hundred other men and things that were then causing the eyes of the world to be turned to Kansas, and the average Kansan will gaze blankly at you, and wonder of what manner of things you are speaking. He can only appreciate and know Kansas history by reading such books as Mrs. Robinson's "Kansas; Its Interior and Exterior Life," Phillips's "Conquest of Kansas by Missouri and her Allies," or Redpath's "Life of John Brown."

2. Again, State pride should induce us to collect Kansas books. The Kansas "spirit" is spoken of all over the country. We are in Kansas because we believe in her, and are not afraid to say so to any and all inquirers.

> "Kansas more, but never less—
> Kansas all the time,"

is our motto. We may bore our friends in the East by our raptures, we may slightly gloss over defects—we wish that they were not here, and presto! they vanish; we may exaggerate, the slightest particle, when we are extolling her merits, but beneath it all there is honest faith and pride in Kansas.

3. Perhaps it will be counted selfish by some, and yet I do not hesitate to say that for the sake of showing our appreciation of the writers of the State, we ought to have a collection of Kansas books. Who have written our books? Usually they have been written by the men and women

who have labored most faithfully as newspaper writers in the interest of our State. It would astonish you to know how many of our books have been written by editors. In the pages of these books is to be found the history of a crime as atrocious as that described by Carlyle, more despicable than that which so aroused the indignation of Victor Hugo. The story they tell is that of —

> "Kansas, most loved of Fortune's guests,
> Child of our hopes and fears;
> Kansas, whose genius ever wrests,
> Victory from Fortune's tears."

And so, as we make the collection and learn the story, our sympathies are broadened, our faculties are energized, and we receive with new faith the old doctrine of the ultimate triumph of right.   J. W. D. ANDERSON.

NOW I LAY ME.

[The Wichita *Eagle* says the following poem was left at the office by an unknown man who came to ask for work.]

Near the camp-fire's flickering light,
  In my blanket bed I lie,
Gazing through the shades of night
  And the twinkling stars on high.
O'er me spirits in the air
  Silent vigils seem to keep,
As I breathe my childhood prayers
  "Now I lay me down to sleep."

Sadly sings the whippoorwill
  In the boughs of yonder tree,
Laughingly the dancing rill
  Swells the midnight melody.

Foeman may be lurking near
 In the cañon dark and deep —
Low I breathe in Jesus' ear
 "I pray the Lord my soul to keep."

Mid those stars one face I see —
 One the Saviour took away —
Mother, who in infancy
 Taught my baby lips to pray.
Her sweet spirit hovers near
 In this lonely mountain brake —
Take me to her Saviour dear,
 "If I should die before I wake."

Fainter grows the flickering light,
 As each ember slowly dies;
Plaintively the birds of night
 Fill the air with sudden cries;
Over me they seem to cry:
 You may never more awake.
Low I lisp: If I should die,
 "I pray the Lord my soul to take."

 "Now I lay me down to sleep;
 I pray the Lord my soul to keep.
 If I should die before I wake,
 I pray the Lord my soul to take."

KANSAS-DAY SONG.

Tune—"*America.*"

God bless our glorious State,
Pride of our nation great,
  Home of the free.
O Kansas, brave and fair!
No State with thee compare;
Thy praises we declare,
  We sing of thee.

When o'er our mighty land,
With a relentless hand,
  Wrong held stern sway,
Then Kansas as a star,
Shone, led as conqueror;
No more can slavery mar,
  Nor bring dismay.

Undaunted, true and brave,
She sent her sons to save
  Her country's name.
A record clear she shows,
That ever brighter grows—
A radiance ever throws
  On page of fame.

God bless our gallant State!
Honored and loved and great,
  Both rich and just.

Her loyal people we,
Beneath her banner free
Rejoice in liberty,
    In God we trust.

                    LAURA E. NEWELL.

THE KANSAS DUGOUT.

Stuck in a Kansas hillside, far away,
Is a cabin built of sod, and made to stay;
    Through the window-like embrasure
    Pours the mingled gold and azure
Of the morning of a gorgeous Kansas day.

Round the cabin, clumps of roses, here and there,
With their mild and welcome fragrance fill the air,
    And the love of heaven settles
    On their pensive pink-lined petals,
As the angels come and put them in their hair.

Blue-eyed children round the cabin chase the day;
They are learning life's best lesson — how to stay,
    To be tireless and restful;
    And the antelope look wistful,
And they want to join the children in their play.

Fortune-wrecked, the parents sought the open West,
Leaving happy homes and friends they love the best;
    Homes in cities bright and busy,
    That responded to the dizzy,
To the whirling and tumultuous unrest.

Oft it happens unto families and men
That they need must touch the mother earth again;
    Rising rugged and reliant,
    Like Antæus, the old giant—
Then they dare and do great things, and not till then.

As around his neck the arms of children twine,
Then the father says: "Have courage, children mine;
    Though the skies around thee blacken,
    Courage!—the gales will slacken,
And the future with its promise shall be thine."

Happy prairie children! Time with rapid wings
To the earnest soul the golden trophy brings.
    As the Trojan said, "Durate
    Vosmet rebus et servate,"
Hold yourselves in hand for higher, nobler things.

                      IRONQUILL.

MIS' SMITH.

All day she hurried to get through,
The same as lots of winmin do;
Sometimes at night her husban' said,
"Ma, ain't you goin' to come to bed?"
And then she'd kinder give a hitch,
And pause half-way between a stitch,
And sorter sigh, and say that she
Was ready as she'd ever be,
            She reckoned.

And so the years went one by one,
And somehow she was never done;
And when the angel said, as how
"Mis' Smith, it's time you rested now,"
She sorter raised her eyes to look
A second, as a stitch she took;
"All right, I'm comin' now," says she;
"I'm ready as I'll ever be,
          I reckon."

ALBERT BIGELOW PAINE.

KANSAS COURAGE.

Kansas does what she starts out to do. No weakness. No hesitation. No timorous shivering on the brink. No retreating. No doubting. No whining. No cowardice. That is why the world loves her.

It would have been easy to cower before border-ruffian-ism and pro-slavery from 1854 to 1860; but Kansas fought. She had started out to establish freedom, and she did it.

It would have been easy, being so far away, to have done little in the War for the Union; Kansas sent soldiers to every battle-field, from the Rio Grande to Gettysburg. She had started out to stand by the Flag, and she did it.

It would have been easy when the war was over to sit down and weep over ruined homes, neglected farms, burned towns, and endless stretches of empty prairie; Kansas went to work. She had started out to build towns and open farms and make homes, and she did it.

When the grasshoppers came, and the drouth, it would have been easy to give up the struggle and go away; Kansas stayed. She had started out to possess the land and to make a living out of it, and she did it.

Other States waited till they were old to build schools and churches and universities and railroads; Kansas built them in her youth. She had started out to make this a place to live, a place fitted up with "all that adorns and embellishes civilized life," and she did it.

Other States have been afraid of the whisky traffic, have not dared to fight it, or after beginning the battle have stopped before it was half won; Kansas took it by the throat and held it until it dropped in a heap, limp and helpless and harmless. She had started out to prohibit the liquor traffic, and she did it.

And thus it has been from the beginning of the book to the end, from the preface to the last page written. Kansas, as they say out West, "Don't fear nothing." The thing she undertakes is the thing she does. The road she starts on is the road she travels. She is never discouraged. She never sulks. She never gets rattled. Steadily, buoyantly, with tireless energy, with the keenest intelligence, with courage that no disaster can daunt, she is climbing to the shining stars.

And the world loves her.

Chas. F. Scott.

THE GATES AJAR.

I have seen a Kansas sunset like a vision in a dream,
When a halo was about me and a glory on the stream;
When the birds had ceased their music and the summer
    day was done,
And prismatic exhalations came a-drifting, from the sun;
And those gold and purple vapors, and the holy stillness
    there,
Lay upon the peaceful valley like a silent evening prayer.
And I've gazed upon that atmospheric splendor of the
    West,
Till it seemed to me a gateway to the regions of the blest.

I have seen a Kansas sunrise like the waking of a dream,
When every dewy blade of grass caught up the golden
    gleam;
When every bird renewed the song he sang the night before,
And all the silent, slumbering world returned to life once
    more;
When every burst of radiance called up a throng of life,
And all the living, waking world with melody was rife.
And as that flood of light and song came floating down
    the plain,
It seemed to me those golden gates were opened wide
    again.

ALBERT BIGELOW PAINE.

HICKORYE CREEK LOGIC.

A wise legislator from Hickorye creek,
Went up to Topeeky to furse an' kick,
An' make 'propriashun bills all look sick;
  An' he was thick
  Ez compressed brick,
This wise legislator from Hickorye creek.

The bill fer the 'Versity ketched his eye,
An' struck him as bein' onusu 'ly high.
"An' twenty-five thousand fer books ! Oh, my !
  Well now, sir, I
  Jes' kaint see why,
They want all them books fer to study by."

"How meny books hev ye got ? " sez he,
"Oh, raisen' ten thousand now," sez we.
"Fer five hundred students.   W 'y geemunee,
  Now that gits me,
  An 'I kain't see
W 'y you don't read w 'at you 've got," sez he.

      FROM "HELIANTHUS ANNUUS."

LITTLE THINGS.

We call him strong who stands unmoved —
 Calm as some tempest-beaten rock —
 When some great trouble hurls its shock;

We say of him, his strength is proved.
 But when the spent storm folds its wings,
 How bears he then life's little things?

About his brow we twine our wreath
 Who seeks the battle's thickest smoke,
 Braves flashing gun and sabre-stroke,
And scoffs at danger, laughs at death :
 We praise him till the whole land rings —
 But is he brave in little things?

But what is life? Drops make the sea;
 And petty cares and small events,
 Small causes and small consequents,
Make up the sum for you and me.
 Then, O for strength to meet the stings
 That arm the points of little things.

ELLEN P. ALLERTON.

JUDGE BREWER ON KANSAS.

In my boyhood's geography, Kansas was put down as a part of the Great American Desert, and yet she has made the wilderness bud and blossom as the rose. But grander far than any material development has been the pathway which she has lined with school-house and church. Go where you will, through her borders, and there stand before you the open doors of the school-house in whose portals stands the ever-present Yankee school-marm — priestess of virtue and prophetess of knowledge and glory; while

the spires of her thousands of churches attest the universal
faith in Him for whose worship our fathers crossed the
sea.   It is no wonder that in the past history of the State
every Kansan glories, and in its future believes.   This is
the home of the modern pilgrim.   Here is the real puritan.
Plymouth Rock has been moved from Massachusetts to
Kansas, and from this State shall henceforth flow the ideas
to rule the continent.   It is honor enough to have lived
in Kansas and been a part of her history.

PAWPAWS RIPE.

The sunny plains of Kansas dozed
    In soft October haze;
The wayside leaves and grass disclosed
    Scarce sign of autumn days.
The corn-stalks bent their ears of gold,
    To list the cricket's din;
And fields of sprouting wheat foretold
    The farmer's laden bin.

Many a mover's caravan
    Stretched westward far away,
As they had moved, since spring began,
    To where the homesteads lay.
Their wagon-sheets were snowy white,
    Their cattle sleek and stout;
Their children's merry faces bright,
    With blooming health shone out.

But ho! what apparition queer
  Is this that looms in sight?
Has Rip Van Winkle wandered here
  Just from his waking plight?
Has one of the Lost Tribes come back,
  With remnant of his band,
And eastward turned once more his track,
  To seek the Promised Land?

Beneath yon shade I 'll sit me there,
  Upon that bank of grass,
And inventory, as it were,
  These nomads, as they pass.
There may be reason wise and strong,
  Unknown to us, why they,
Of all the steady moving throng,
  Are on the backward way.

A wagon of past ages, built
  On model lost to art;
A dirty, ragged, faded quilt
  Supplied a cover's part.
Wheels of four sizes, tireless now,
  With many a missing spoke;
A three-legged mule, a one-horned cow,
  Tugged slowly in the yoke.

A man of five-and-forty years,
  With beard of grizzled brown;
A brimless hat sat on his ears,
  His hair strayed through the crown;

His pants of dingy butternut,
  His coat of tarnished blue,
His feet with no incumbrance but
  Mismated boot and shoe.

Six hungry curs of low degree
  Sneaked at their master's heels,
Or, underneath the axle-tree,
  Kept measure with the wheels.
Packed in the feeding-box behind,
  A time-worn jug is spied,
Whose corn-cob stopper hints the kind
  Of nourishment inside.

Nine boys and girls with rheumy eyes,
  Stowed in with beds and tins,
Were all so nearly of a size,
  They might have well been twins.
The mother, as a penance sore
  For loss of youth and hope,
Seemed to have vowed, long years before,
  To fast from comb and soap.

"Halloo, my friend! a brood like that
  Should head the other way;
The land is broad, and free, and fat—
  Go take it while you may."
Raising his glazed and dirty sleeve,
  He gave his mouth a wipe,
And answered, with a sighing heave:
  "Stranger, pawpaws is ripe!

"Do n't tell me of your corn and wheat —
    What do I care for sich ?
Do n't say your schools is hard to beat,
    And Kansas soil is rich.
Stranger, a year 's been lost by me,
    Searchin' your Kansas siles,
And not a pawpaw did I see,
    For miles, and miles, and miles !

"Missouri 's good enough for me ;
    The bottom timber 's wide ;
The best of livin' thar is free,
    And spread on every side.
In course, the health ain't good for some,
    But we 're not of that stripe,
Hey! Bet and Tobe! we 're gwien home !
    Git up!   Pawpaws is ripe ! "

He cracked his whip, and off they went,
    The mule and cow, and dogs.
I watched them till they all were blent
    With distant haze and fogs ;
And as the blue smoke heavenward curled
    Up from his corn-cob pipe,
He dreamed not of that better world,
    For here pawpaws were ripe !

                        Sol. Miller.

KANSAS.

(A RECITATION.)

Would you like to hear me say
My lesson in geography?
Listen, then, while I begin it;
I can give you all that's in it;
Ever word I want to tell —
Teacher says I know it well.

Kansas! born amid the strife
Menacing a Nation's life,
In the crimson tide baptized —
Blood of martyrs' sacrificed —
Struggling, battling, growing strong
In her ceaseless strife with wrong,
Yielding never in the fight
Till the victory of right,
Kansas stands among her mates
One of these United States;
North, Nebraska State is found,
Missouri is her eastern bound
South, the Nation greets our eyes,
And Colorado westward lies.

Time would fail to speak her praises,
Tell her worth and what she raises;
Corn and cotton, grains and grasses,
Peanuts, castor-beans, molasses,
Fruit of all kinds, nuts, persimmons,
Gallant men and handsome women.

To the stars through clouds she rises,
Conquering foes in all disguises ;
Cyclones threaten desolation ;
Flood and fire bring devastation ;
Grasshoppers have tried to eat her ;
Whisky rings would fain defeat her ;
But, borne onward, upward ever,
May her banner waver never.

MAGGIE A. KILMER.

SUNFLOWER SONG.

TUNE — "*Golden Slippers.*"

[NOTE.—Arrange a white screen with holes cut the size of children's
faces ; paint yellow leaves on screen around margin of holes ; place real
sunflower stalks in front of screen, or make them of sticks or weeds
covered with green paper. Children sing Sunflower Song with faces in
holes forming center of sunflowers.]

Most all the sunflowers are faded away,
And they do n't 'spect to shine till a warmer day,
And our broad green leaves that we loved so well
Will be gathered for the farmer in the morning,
And the long green stalks that we had last June
All got changed 'cause it frosted so soon.
And the green old earth that we used to see
We will all have to leave in the morning.

CHORUS :

Oh ! dear golden sunflowers,
Oh ! dear golden sunflowers,
Golden sunflowers that 's gwine away,
Becase they can't look sweet.

Oh! dear golden sunflowers,
Oh! dear golden sunflowers,
Golden sunflowers that 's gwine away,
Becase they can't look sweet.

All our óld brethren hang on the wall,
'Cause it haint been warm since away last fall,
But we flowers all think we 'll have a good time
When we see Oscar Wilde in the morning.
The big red rose and the flower-de-luce
Will telegraph the news to the tall green spruce;
What a grand display there will be that day,
When we see Oscar Wilde in the morning.
                    Chorus.

So it 's good-bye all; we have to go
Where the frost don't come and the wind don't blow,
For our colors bright we cannot keep
If we stay where it freezes in the morning.
But our golden rays must be nice and clean
And our age must be just right to lean
Our head upon his broad lapel,
When we see Oscar Wilde in the morning.
                    Chorus.
                                    [ANONYMOUS.]

A TRIBUTE TO JOHN BROWN.

[NOTE. — Read at a reception given at Topeka in honor of Mrs. Mary
A. Brown, widow of John Brown.]

Against this crime of crimes he fought and fell;
He freed a race and found a prison cell;
In mid-air hung upon the gibbet's tree,
But lived and died, thank God, to make men free.

And dusky men the ages down will tell,
For what he fought, and how he bravely fell;
And dim the jewels in each earthly crown,
Beside the luster of·thy name, John Brown.

J. G. WATERS.

A FARMER'S WIFE.

"Ellen P. Allerton, the Kansas poet of much fame, is
a modest farmer's wife. She writes gracefully, and has
written from childhood. Her thoughts are lofty. She is
plain in dress and manner. She is never affected. She is
fond of flowers and pretty things. She is a woman true
men admire. When the Allertons bought a farm near
Hiawatha, Mrs. Allerton worked very hard with her husband to pay for it, writing little, for writing doesn't pay.
Now they are out of debt, have a snug home, with orchards, stock, good crops, and time to write. Mrs. Allerton's
poems were printed in a small book some time ago.
Enough copies have been sold to pay for printing.

"Her first poem was childish prattle about a yellow dog. When she had grown older she sent verses to the New York *Tribune*, and they were printed by Horace Greeley, who praised them.

"Mrs. Allerton's 'Walls of Corn' and Mr. Ware's 'Washerwoman's Song' are the best known and most widely circulated poems.

"Mrs. Allerton's rhymes are musical, and her thought is always encouraging. She is never gloomy. She does not plow so deep as some, but there is more of her golden grain in the market."

EWING HERBERT.

SING A SONG OF KANSAS.

Sing a song of Kansas,
Princess of the West,
One of many sisters —
Fairest one, and best.

Heart of a great nation,
Brilliant central star,
Seen of all observers,
Hailed from near and far.

Stately in proportions,
Giantess in size,
Noted for her climate,
Famous for her skies.

Marvelous in progress,
Wonderful in deeds,
Other States may follow,
Kansas ever leads.

Sing a song of Kansas,
Land of fruit and grain ;
Sound aloud her praises,
Thunder the refrain.

— *Emporia Republican.*

KANSAS.

Kansas corn and Kansas wheat,
  Kansas rye and oats,
Kansas sugar-cane and beets,
  Kansas steers and shoats ;
Kansas air and Kansas soil,
  Kansas sunñy skies,
Kansas grit and Kansas toil,
  Kansas enterprise ;
Kansas mines and Kansas mills,
  Kansas brawn and brain,
Kansas valleys, plains, and hills,
  Kansas sun and rain ;
Kansas homes and Kansas farms,
  Kansas fruits and shades,
Kansas schools and Kansas marms,
  Kansas buxom maids ;

Kansas culture, Kansas wealth,
  Kansas iron rails,
Kansas climate, Kansas health,
  Kansas empty jails,
Kansas books and Kansas press,
  Kansas prose and rhyme :
Kansas more, but never less —
  Kansas all the time.

W. F. CRAIG.

RESUBMISSION.

Who asks for resubmission of the law of prohibition?
  Who signs the great petition which before our gaze
      unrolls?
Are the Kansas people tiring of the spirit that was firing
  Their souls when that great army triumphant swept the
      polls?

Who asks for resubmission of the law of prohibition?
  Is the question that is coming from the East and from
      the West;
And the South with many voices, and the freedman that
      rejoices,
    And the anxious and the waiting, ask : "Will Kansas
        bear the test?"

Has the mother grown aweary for the watches long and
      dreary?   .
  When the hours dragged to midnight and were mingled
      with her prayers

For the weak one who was trying, all his tempter's rules
    defying,
  To run the dreaded gauntlet of the wine-shop and its
    snares?

Does the glad wife long to listen, her eyes with tears
    aglisten,
  For the husband staggering homeward from the revel
    at the dawn?
Or the maiden under cover of the gloaming wait her lover,
  Till her heart is worn and anxious and its restfulness is
    gone?

Does the man with altered manner marching under this
    great banner,
  Self-supporting, self-respecting, calm, reliant, strong and
    brave,
Want his boys to face the danger? Does he ask it for
    the stranger,
  That he bury all his manhood in a sot's dishonored
    grave?

Are the men and women turning to the streets for pau-
    pers yearning?
  Do they want to fill asylums and their prisons' empty
    cells?
Do they want the drunkard reeling by them without sense
    of feeling?
  The saloon whose gilded glamour but conceals a thou-
    sand hells?

Who wants this resubmission? Who swells this great peti-
     tion
That unrolls before the Senate its panoply of names;
Men and women consecrating life to truth, not hesitating,
     Or the wily politician who debases and defames?

Rise up, O noble people! let the bells from every steeple
     Ring the triumph and the glory of the right above the
          wrong;
Ye who fought for federation, for the freedom of the
     Nation,
     Steady, now, for prohibition, more than half a million
          strong!

All the world that rang your praises, at your danger
     breathless gazes;
     Every man who loves his brother; every soul that from
          its clod
Of unputrified ambition, bursts its chrysalis condition,
     And soars outward, onward, upward, on the wings of
          faith and God.

Who asks for resubmission of the law of prohibition?
     Is the question that is coming from the East and from
          the West;
And the South with many voices, and the freedman who
     rejoices,
     Answer, "Kansas never failed us; she is sure to bear
          the test."
                                        EMMA P. SEABURY.

JOHN BROWN'S LAST SPEECH.

I have, may it please the court, a few words to say.

In the first place, I deny everything but what I have all along admitted — the design on my part to free the slaves. I intended certainly to have made a clean thing of that matter, as I did last winter, when I went into Missouri and there took slaves without the snapping of a gun on either side, moved them through the country, and finally left them in Canada. I designed to have done the same thing again, on a larger scale. That was all I intended. I never intended murder, or treason, or destruction, or to excite slaves to rebellion, or to make insurrection. I have another objection, and that is, it is unjust that I should suffer such a penalty. Had I interfered, in the manner which I admit, and which I admit has been fairly proved, (for I admire the truthfulness and candor of the greater portion of the witnesses who have testified in this case,) had I so interfered in behalf of the rich, the powerful, the intelligent, the so-called great, or in behalf of any of their friends, either father, mother, brother, sister, wife, or children, or any of that class, and suffered and sacrificed what I have in this interference, it would have been all right; and every man in this court would have deemed it an act worthy of reward rather than punishment. Now if it is deemed necessary that I should forfeit my life for the furtherance of the ends of justice, and mingle my blood further with the blood of my children and with the blood of millions in this slave country whose rights are disregarded by wicked, cruel and unjust enactments, I submit; so let it be done.

—*Sanborn's "Life and Letters of John Brown."*

DON'T YOU TELL.

If you have a cherished secret,
    Don't you tell :—
Not your friend, for his tympanum
    Is a bell,
With its echoes wide-rebounding,
Multiplied and far-resounding,—
    Don't you tell.

If yourself, you cannot keep it,
    Then, who can?
Could you more expect of any
    Other man?
Yet you put him, if he tells it,
If he gives away or sells it,
    Under ban.

Sell your gems to any buyer
    In the mart;
Of your wealth to feed the hungry,
    Spare a part.
Blessings on the open pocket;
But your secret, keep it, lock it,
    In your heart.

                MRS. ALLERTON.

THE SOD SCHOOL-HOUSE.

THE SOD SCHOOL-HOUSE.

An earthern mound on the prairie's swell,
  The work of rough settlers' hands,
An uncouth temple for learning made,
Its walls of the rudest earth-squares laid—
  A lone sod school-house stands.

Not a tree in sight from the open door,
  Not a shrub on the landscape's face,
But a sea of grass fills all the view;
Its waves are of emerald's sparkling hue,
  And above cloud-shadows race.

I hear the sound of a tinkling bell;
  'Tis the teacher's signal sweet.
There's a drowsy hum from a score of lips,
There's a smothered laugh at some dullard's slips,
  And a noise of restless feet.

Do they think as they tread the earthen floor,
  Those children gathered there,
How near to nature's true heart they stand,
Their tan-stained cheeks by her light breath fanned,
  Their eyes on her features fair?

Do they hear the notes forever new,
  That the limitless prairies sing?
'Tis a nobler strain than books have told,
Than choirs have breathed, or organs rolled,
  Or silver chimes can ring.

They say, "Be pure as our morning dew,
　　Be firm as our leagues of earth,
Be kind as our breezes that gently blow,
Be bright as our hills in the sunset's glow,
　　Be gay as our song-bird's mirth.

"Look up to the light like the spears that wave
　　O'er all our stretching miles;
Let the flowers that dimple our bosom cast
A spell of beauty that shall at last
　　Tinge manhood's years with smiles."

And the peaceful haze at yonder rim,
　　Just kissing the prairie sea,
Has a soft refrain for the song of life—
It whispers, "Beyond this earthly strife
　　Lies the glorious rest to be."

Can the youthful ears but catch the hymn,
　　Can the hearts its lesson glean,
With what wealth of soul to the world they'll go
From that earth-walled school-room cramped and low,
　　'Mid the hills of lustrous green.

CHARLES MOREAU HARGER.

(In Frost's Collections.)

THE WORLD A SCHOOL.

"Young men, young women, crowding forward from the
byways into the broad highway of life, may you do well the
work which is waiting for your hands, realizing the obliga-
tion spoken of by Lord Bacon: 'I hold every man a debtor

to his profession; from the which, as men of course do seek to receive countenance and profit, so ought they of duty to endeavor themselves by way of amends to be a help and ornament thereunto.'

"May your lives resemble not the desert's bitter stream, which mocks the cracked and blistered lips of the fainting, dying traveler; which but adds horror to the fiery desert, and sinks at last into the burning sands, to which it brought no verdure, no gladness, from which it received nothing but poison and a grave.

"May the course of your lives find no counterpart in the sluggish course of the dull bayou, a fungus among streams, which winds and doubles and winds again through miles of rank vegetation which curtain its dark course and shut out from its sullen waters the gladsome light of day; but may your lives be like the river which rises amid the pure snows of the bold mountain; which forces its way through the rocks that would impede it in search for the valley; which slakes as it goes the thirst of the deer, and washes the roots of the pine-tree from which the flag of the far-sailing merchantman is yet to fly; which turns the rude wheel of the mountain mill and whirls in its eddies the gathering sawdust as it speeds from under the whirring, glittering teeth of steel it has bidden to rend the logs it has brought them. It grows wider and deeper and more silent, and yet stronger as it flows between smiling farms and thrifty villages, which owe their existence to the bounteous river. At night it sends its mist over all the valley and half-way up the hills, like sweet Charity who silently wraps in her sheltering mantle all the sons of men. It carries on its bosom all floating craft — the light canoe, the slow-drifting raft, the arrow-like steamer. In time its wave-

lcts give back at night in dancing gleams the thousand
lights of the great cotton mills, and anon its waters part
before the prow of the new-built ship as she glides down
the ways to the element which is henceforth to be her
home. Thus goes the shining river, the ever-useful, ever-
blessed river; best friend of toiling man; fairest thing
from the creative hand of God. Thus goes the river, to
mingle at last forever with the sunlit sea."

Noble L. Prentis.

JOHN BROWN.

States are not great
Except as men may make them;
Men are not great except they do and dare.
But States, like men,
Have destinies that take them —
That bear them on, not knowing why or where.

The Why repels
The philosophic searcher —
The Why and Where all questionings defy,
Until we find,
Far back in youthful nurture,
Prophetic facts that constitute the Why.

All merit comes
From daring the unequal;
All glory comes from daring to begin.
Fame loves the State
That, reckless of the sequel,
Fights long and well, though it may lose or win.

Than in our State
No illustration apter
Is seen or found of faith, and hope, and will.
Take up her story:
Every leaf and chapter
Contains a record that conveys a thrill.

And there is one
Whose faith, whose fight, whose failing,
Fame yet shall placard on the walls of time.
He dared begin —
Despite the unavailing;
He dared begin, when failure was a crime.

When over Africa
Some future cycle
Shall sweep the lake-gemmed uplands with its surge;
When, as with trumpet
Of Archangel Michael,
Culture shall bid a colored race emerge;

When busy cities
There, in constellations,
Shall gleam with spires, and palaces, and domes,
With marts wherein
Are heard the noise of nations;
With summer groves surrounding stately homes —

There, future orators
To cultured freemen
Shall tell of valor, and recount with praise
Stories of Kansas,
And of Lacedæmon —
Cradles of freedom, then of ancient days.

From boulevards
O'erlooking both Nyanzas,
The statured bronze shall glitter in the sun,
With rugged lettering:
"JOHN BROWN, OF KANSAS:
HE DARED BEGIN; HE LOST, BUT, LOSING, WON."

EUGENE F. WARE.

THE COYOTE.

He has been called an "outcast" by a notorious poet. He is universally conceded to be a sneak, a thief, and an arrant coward. He is a worthless vagabond, a wanderer o' nights and a lier-by day; a dissipated wretch in whose whole history there is not one redeeming fact. He has an extensive connection but no family. He is disowned by the dogs, and not recognized by respectable foxes. He will lengthen out the days of his life until his voice sounds hollow and thin and aged, in the watches of the night. Nothing less than infinite pains and insidious strychnine will end his vagabond life. As his gray back moves slowly along at a leisurely trot, above the reeds and coarse grass, and he turns his sly face over his shoulder to regard you, he knows immediately whether or not you have with you your gun. The coyote is a reflecttive brute and has an inquiring mind, and he proceeds to interview you, in a way which for politeness and unobtrusiveness is recommended as a model to more intelligent and scarcely less obtrusive animals. As he sits himself complacently down upon his tail at the summit of the

nearest knoll, and lolls his red tongue, and seems to wink
in your direction, he is so much like his cousin the dog,
that you can hardly refrain from whistling to him. Make
any hostile demonstration and he moves a few paces
further and sits down again. Lie down in the grass and
remain quiet for an hour, and by slyly watching him from
the corner of your eye you will discover that he has been
joined by a half-dozen of his brethren and friends. He
is conscious of the frailty of life and now wants to find
out, first, if you are dead; and second, supposing you are
not, if there is anything else in your neighborhood which
is eatable. You rise up in sudden indignation and scare
the committee away. In that case you have offended the
coyote family deeply, and they retire to a safe distance
and bark ceaselessly until they have hooted you out of the
neighborhood.

He is a brute which is entitled to respect from his very
persistence in knavery. Contemptible in person and count-
less in numbers, he forages fatness from things despised
of all others.

Like all cowards, he can fight desperately when he
must, and the borderer's dogs wear many an ugly scar of
his making. Winter and summer, in heat and cold, he
wags his way along the prairie path with the same droop-
ing, quick-turning, watchful head; the same lolling red
tongue, the same bushy tail trailing behind; ever-mindful
of a coyote's affairs, ever looking for supper; the figure-
head, the feature, the representative of the broad and
silent country of which he comes more nearly being
master than any other.

—*Extracts from Steele's "Sons of the Border."*

QUIVERA — KANSAS.

1542-1882.

In that half forgotten era,
　With the avarice of old,
　Seeking cities that were told
　To be paved with solid gold,
In the kingdom of Quivera.

Came the restless Coronado
　To the open Kansas plain,
　With his knights from sunny Spain ;
　In an effort that, though vain,
Thrilled with boldness and bravado.

League by league, in aimless marching,
　Knowing scarcely where or why,
　Crossed the uplands drear and dry,
　That an unprotected sky
Had for centuries been parching.

But their expectations, eager,
　Found, instead of fruitful lands,
　Shallow streams and shifting sands,
　Where the buffalo in bands
Roamed o'er deserts dry and meager.

Back to scenes more trite, yet tragic,
　Marched the knights with armor'd steeds;
　Not for them the quiet deeds;
　Not for them to sow the seeds
From which empires grow like magic.

Never land so hunger-stricken
  Could a Latin race remold;
  They could conquer heat or cold —
  Die for glory or for gold —
But not make a desert quicken.

Thus Quivera was forsaken;
  And the world forgot the place,
  Until centuries apace
  Came the blue-eyed Saxon race,
And it bade the desert waken.

And it bade the climate vary;
  And awaiting no reply
  From the elements on high,
  It with plows besieged the sky —
Vexed the heavens with the prairie.

Then the vitreous sky relented,
  And the unacquainted rain
  Fell upon the thirsty plain,
  Whence had gone the knights of Spain,
Disappointed, discontented.

Sturdy are the Saxon faces,
  As they move along in lines;
  Bright the rolling-cutters shine,
  Charging up the State's incline,
As an army storms a glacis.

Into loam the sand is melted,
  And the blue-grass takes the loam,
  Round about the prairie home;
  And the locomotives roam
Over landscapes iron-belted.

Cities grow where stunted birches
 Hugged the shallow water-line,
 And the deepening rivers twine
 Past the factory and mine,
Orchard slopes and schools and churches.

Deeper grows the soil, and truer;
 More and more the prairie teems
 With a fruitage as of dreams;
 Clearer, deeper, flow the streams,
Blander grows the sky, and bluer.

We have made the State of Kansas,
 And to-day she stands complete—
 First in freedom, first in wheat;
 And her future years will meet
Riper hopes and richer stanzas.

EUGENE F. WARE.

THE TRAIL OF "49."

Across the prairie where I dwell
Stretches away from swell to swell,
A road that might a story tell.

The track is wide, and deeply cut
By wheels of heavy wagons, but
The rank grass grows in seam and rut.

'Tis the old trail of "Forty-nine";
Thus history, in graven line,
Has stamped this prairie home of mine,

Tracing it where it winds away,
There comes to me, at twilight gray,
A vision of another day.

I see the covered wagons go
Across the prairie, toiling slow,
Through dreary storms, through summer glow.

I see them with their human freight,
Hearts throbbing high with hopes elate,
Pass onward to a doubtful fate.

Months pass; a weary, jaded train,
Worn with fatigue, disease, and pain,
Creeps slowly o'er a desert plain.

Above, a cloudless, burning sky;
Below, naught greets the weary eye,
Save wastes of sand and alkali.

No rains descend, no water flows;
No cool trees bend, no green thing grows:
Yet still that sad train onward goes.

Fatigue and thirst! no tongue can tell
The victim's anguish, fierce and fell —
His fondest dream, a bubbling well.

And some go mad and wildly rave;
Some find what, at the last, they crave —
The silence of a desert grave.

The living speak in husky tones;
The poor brutes drop with piteous moans;
The track is paved with bleaching bones.

Still onward, slower and more slow,
Dogged nightly by a stealthy foe,
Toward mountain passes choked with snow.

One sleeps to dream of home and wife;
He wakes, at call of midnight strife
With tomahawk and scalping-knife.

. . . .

Past perils, miseries untold;
Past desert's heat, past mountain cold —
What waits them in the land of gold?

Go, search a checkered history,
Of soon-got hoards, as soon to flee;
Of princely wealth and poverty.

Go search them all, through every line,
Yet deign to read this song of mine,
Of the old trail of "Forty-nine."

MRS. ALLERTON.

TO KANSAS.

Not for thy outward charms of form and face,
  Careful to leave no feature unexpressed,
    As if for beauty's sake we love thee best,
We bring the praise; nor for thy pride of race,
Nor for thy wealth that waxeth great apace;
  Nor will we vaunt, with low and swinish zest,
    The milky richness of thy mother-breast,
Like unweaned babes that know no higher grace.

Shall we be lured by these things? Are not we
A something more than mouth, and eyes, and ears,
   To eat, and look, and listen life away?
More than these skin-deep beauties must thou be,
   To win and keep our homage through the years;
Yea, fair in more transcendent wise than they.

And fair thou art, as we would have thee be,
   Fair even in this more transcendent wise;
   The light of high communings on thee lies;
Thy touch the bond abide not, but are free,
Thy look is gracious, holy; none but thee,
   Smiled on how e'er she be by happy skies,
   Hath power to still the hunger of our eyes,
Unsated by the mountains and the sea.

For thou art Freedom's daughter, and thy birth
Was through the pain of Righteousness' wars;
   Thy cradle-song, the battle's roar and din.
Therefore thy beauty hath the greater worth
   Of nobler thoughts; so art thou fair within,
And claimest thine the pathway of the stars.

ARTHUR GRAVES CANFIELD.
(In Frost's Collection.)

"GOD SAVE OUR TOWN."

Beyond the sea in cities old,
With time-worn walls and moss-grown towers,
Still, as we are by travelers told,
The ancient watchman calls the hours;
At midnight, when the moon rides high,
Rings out his voice to the roofs and sky,
"Twelve o'clock, twelve o'clock, and all's well.
    God save our town."

But scarce his voice has died away
Ere from the great cathedral down
Midst the sculptured saints who pray all day,
Rings out o'er the sleeping town
The pealing voice of the mighty bell,
"All's well, all's well.
    God save our town."

And thus the carrier comes to-day,
Like the old watchman far away,
And thus to each and all doth say:
    From flood, from fire,
    From battle's ire,
    From earthquake's harm,
    From rage of storm,
    From pestilence that walks abroad,
    And spreads its flight,
    By noon and night,
      God save our town.

From pride that scorns a neighbor poor,
Or drives a beggar from his door;
From misers hoarding up their gold,
From rascals cunning, bright, or bold—
Each in their several degree,
And from the loud-voiced Pharisee,
    God save our town.
      —From N. L. Prentis' Carrier's Address.

KANSAS.

(FOR A PICTURE.)

A gracious figure, clad in living green,
  Enwrought with gold, and broidered thick with
    flowers,
  A woman, strong in woman's noblest powers,
Who holds the scepter of a fearless queen,
And there is love in her blue eyes, I ween—
  The love that keeps a watch from its own towers,
  And on her lips the purpose that endowers
Her royal children with her royal sheen!

Above her floats a gonfalon, unfurled,
  That men may see her colors from afar,
And read therein her message to the world;
  Steadfast she stands, be it in peace or war,
Nor falters not though heavy clouds be hurled
  Athwart the glory of her guiding star.

                FLORENCE L. SNOW.
                  (In Frost's Collection.)

THE STATE REFORM SCHOOL.

Here, under the care and guidance of faithful and conscientious officers and teachers, the unfortunate boys of our State, who, from force of circumstances or an inherited tendency to wrong-doing, have taken the first step toward a criminal life, are subjected to a discipline mildly but firmly administered, and a moral, mental and physical training that is designed and executed with a view to the formation of good character, with all that that implies.

Upon approaching the school, the boy, whose dreams have been disturbed by visions of gloomy, prison-like walls, barred windows, and the rattle of bolts and chains, is surprised to see a beautiful, well-kept lawn and attractive buildings, with nothing suggesting a prison. He enters, after ascending a short flight of broad stone steps, and is conducted to the office. Here he is questioned as to his past life, his standing in the common-school branches, his habits, good and bad, and such facts as might give some insight into his character. He is then taken to the bath-room, and after bathing is provided with the regulation uniform. This is cadet gray, with brass buttons and military cap. He receives two suits — one for Sunday and one for every-day wear. Now, after being assigned to one of the four divisions or families into which the inmates are divided, he becomes a full member of this busy little community.

Like all his companions, he has been committed to the care of the State until he is twenty-one years old, but he is informed that by good conduct he may earn the privilege of returning to home and friends in a comparatively short time—possibly in 15 months, though it is probable that his stay will be about 30, the average time of the 500 boys who had been discharged up to June 30, 1892, being 29 months.

Let us follow the boys through one day of their school life. At 5:30 A. M. the rising-bell rings. After dressing, each boy makes his own bed. At a signal from the officer they march to the school-room, where they have a short devotional exercise, closing with the Lord's Prayer recited in unison. From here they pass to the play-ground, if the weather permits, if not, to the play-room, and remain until 6:15. They then move to the lavatory and prepare for the morning meal. After breakfast, they all assemble for the detail, and the different classes are sent to their morning's work. Part of them go to school and others to the various departments—as the tailor shop, shoe shop, laundry, engine room, kitchens, dining rooms, dormitories, farm, etc. Work ceases at 11:30, and the preparations for dinner are the same as for breakfast. At 1 P. M. comes detail again. Those who were in school in the morning will now be required to do the work, while those who worked in the morning will have their turn in school. The departments close at 5:30, and supper is ready at 6. Between supper and sundown, the time is spent in play. Once more in the school-room, the officer credits those against whom there are no charges, with one day of good conduct, while any that are found guilty of misdemeanors will lose one day or more, according to the nature of the offense. From this until bed-time, they will study the Sunday-school lesson, or have books and papers and quiet indoor amusements.

Saturday afternoon is a half-holiday, during which all take a good bath.

On Sunday morning there is a Sabbath-school service, and in the afternoon they listen to a sermon delivered by a minister from the city.

All the national holidays are observed, and through the winter a series of entertainments, in which the music is furnished by their own band and orchestra, provides wholesome and instructive amusement.

The new boy will probably chafe under what to him appears to be unnecessarily strict discipline, but in a short time he finds that it is not so difficult to comply with the regulations as he had fancied. He will begin to do right, possibly from no higher motive than to save his time. But with right-doing comes a feeling of self-respect that in time begets a desire to do right for the sake of right. This desire once awakened, he enters upon the struggle common to all mankind — the fight between conscience and the inclination to do evil. He may stumble, and sometimes fall, but his efforts entitle him to our sympathy and charity.

W. E. Fagan.

KANSAS — RETROSPECTIVE.

Where once the Indian pitched his tent
· Beside the winding river;
Or with a bow slung 'cross his back
(And arrows in a quiver)

Gave chase unto the buffalo,
   Once monarch of the green —
All this, and more transpired, before
   The paleface here was seen.

'Twas then the "noble reds" held sway,
   And with Waunita's hand
To guide them on, they 've gone to view
   Their happy hunting land.
Where wigwams stood, now stands a school,
   To educate the young ;
Where pipes of peace were smoked by chiefs,
   A city since has sprung.

Where once the cactus blooms put forth,
   Beneath a warm sun's rays,
The prairie dogs and rattlesnakes,
   In peace lived all their days.
Now these have gone, and in their place
   A wheat-field is instead,
And every year it brings forth fruit,
   That the hungry may be fed.

Who found her first ?   This is a point
   In dispute between two men.
In fifteen hundred forty-one,
   One says it was — and then
The other fellow's tale comes 'long
   To prove one in a mix,
Declaring he himself was here
   In fifteen thirty-six.

The wealth now shown within our lines,
  'Twere vain it all to state ;
Her churches, schools, corn-fields, and all,
  Would make an empire great.
Our motto hangs on Heaven's walls ;
  Though blazoned with our wars,
It ne'er shone brighter than to-day —
  "Through difficulties to the stars."

GEORGE A. ROOT.

DEATH OF THE SPANISH THREE HUNDRED.
KANSAS, 1721.

Three hundred souls from Santa Fé,
  In that far-off time,
Sought homes where the prairie rivers run,
Under the face of a Kansas sun,
In a beauteous land, and a wild
  But beauteous clime.

Three hundred souls of old Castile,
  The pride of Spain ;
Wives and mothers, sisters, children, sires,
Gathered around the evening fires,
And talked of tender cares, and homes
  Upon the plains.

Three hundred souls of a proud old race,
  Whose soldier hands
Unfurled the flag of the Spanish Cross

In the face of the ocean Albatross,
And braved the unknown waters
    To conquer western lands.

Three hundred souls, in search of homes;
    The mail-clad knights
Were young and strong and battle-tried,
And to the future looked with pride,
Where conquered fields stood out
    Redeemed by a hundred fights.

Three hundred souls — the saintly priest
    Who led them on
Dreamed that the ark of God should stand
To bless his work in the Kansas land,
And the Indian savage from his
    Bloody rites be won.

Three hundred souls, in the face of death —
    The savage foe,
Circling around them — the mail-clad breasts
Defend their own, and many crests
Of hero fame go down in death
    Beneath the Indian blow.

Three hundred souls — soldiers in mail —
    Children, mothers, wives —
Perished that day where they fighting stood,
And died, as became their proud old blood,
In fight — and fame bids live
    The glory of Spanish lives.

Three hundred souls of the olden time
　　Float down the years;
The last wild shriek of that stricken band
Going down in death in Quivera land,
Still afrights the wild bird
　　When gloom of night appears.

Three hundred souls—the wild flowers bloom,
　　Where then they fell;
At times there are sounds on the prairie gale,
Of prayers, and shouts, and dash of mail
Like a last death-fight—then all is still:
　　Time guards his secret well.

JOHN MADDEN.

ORIGINAL PACKAGE.

"What is as an 'Original package,' my dear?"
　　She laid down her paper to ask;
"What is all the rout and the fussing about?
　　To read is too much of a task."

He gave her a glance of amusement and scorn,
　　A way husbands have, don't deny:
"'Tis a package of freight that is sent by one State
　　To another one, when it is dry."

"Oh, yes, to be sure," with a sip of her tea,
　　"To irrigate arable land;
Yet I can but reflect, 'tis odd to object—
　　That is all that I don't understand."

EMMA P. SEABURY.

THE WHISTLING ENGINEER.

Down through the Neosho valley
  There runs an engineer,
With an arm that 's strong and steady,
  With a heart that knows no fear; -
And when his train approaches
  The town where his sweetheart dwells,
He gives a loud, long whistle,
  And thus his presence tells.

It may be in the morning,
  As through his gates of gold
The King of Day approaches
  And scatters wealth untold.
On the fresh, free air it cometh,
  To every listening ear —
The long, long, long shrill whistle
  Of the loving engineer.

Perhaps it is at midnight,
  When darkness like a pall,
With many a wild, weird phantom,
  Has settled over all;
The stillness then is broken,
  And the startled atmosphere
Rings out with the loud, long whistle
  Of the loving engineer.

No matter where the maiden,
  And whether eve or morn,

The sound of that long whistle
  Is like the bugle-horn
Of a gallant Alpine lover;
  It fills her heart with cheer,
And listening to its echoes
  Says: "There's my engineer."

May many years of "running"
  Come to lover and to maid;
May they never need a "wrecker,"
  And never run down grade.
And when these two together
  Approach the other sphere,
May it be with the long, glad whistle
  Of the loving engineer.

J. M. CAVANESS.

JOHN BROWN'S PARALLELS.

"TRADING POST, KANSAS, January, 1859.

"GENTLEMEN': You will greatly oblige a humble friend by allowing the use of your columns while I briefly state two parallels, in my poor way.

"Not one year ago, eleven quiet citizens of this neigh_borhood, viz., William Robertson, William Colpetzer, Amos Hall, Austin Hall, John Campbell, Asa Snyder, William A. Stillwell, William Hairgrove, Asa Hairgrove, Patrick Ross, and B. L. Reed, were gathered up from their work and their homes by an armed force under one Hamilton, and, without trial or opportunity to speak in their own defense, were formed into line, and all but one shot—five killed and five wounded. One fell unharmed, pretending to be dead. All were left for dead. The only crime charged against them was that of being Free-State men. Now, I inquire, what action has ever, since the occurrence in May last, been taken by either the President of the United States, the Governor of Missouri, the Governor of Kansas, or any of their tools, or by any pro-slavery or administration man, to ferret out and punish the perpetrators of this crime?

"Now for the other parallel. On Sunday, December 19th, a negro man called Jim came over to the Osage settlement from Missouri and stated that he, together with his wife, two children, and another negro man, was to be sold within a day or two, and begged for help to get away. On Monday (the following) night, two small companies were made up to go to Missouri and forcibly liberate the five slaves, together with other slaves. One of these companies I assumed to direct. We proceeded to the place, surrounded the buildings, liberated the slaves, and also took certain property supposed to belong to the estate.

"We however learned before leaving that a portion of the articles we had taken belonged to a man living on the plantation as a tenant, and who was supposed to have no interest in the estate. We promptly returned to him all we had taken. We then went to another plantation, where we found five more slaves, took some property and two white men. We moved all slowly away into the Territory for some distance, and then sent the white men back, telling them to follow us as soon as they chose to do so. The other company freed one female slave, took some property, and, as I am informed, killed one white man (the master), who fought against the liberation.

"Now for a comparison. Eleven persons are forcibly restored to their natural and inalienable rights, with but one man killed. . . . It is currently reported that the Governor of Missouri has made requisition upon the Governor of Kansas for the delivery of all such as were concerned in the last-named 'dreadful outrage.' The Marshal of Kansas is said to be collecting a posse of Missouri (not Kansas) men at West Point, in Missouri, a little town about ten miles distant, to "enforce the laws.' All pro-slavery, conservative Free-State and dough-face men, and administration tools, are filled with holy horror.

"Consider the two cases, and the action of the administration party.   Respectfully yours,

JOHN BROWN."

THE CYCLONE OF MAY 27, 1892.

Wind of a Kansas plain,
    Breathing through fragrant bowers,
Whispering of sun and rain,
    Kissing the dew from the flowers;
Over the grain-fields' billowy waves,
    Lifting the leaves of the growing corn;
On past the gorge's rock-bound caves,
    Where the howling imps of the storm are born.
        Hark to its roar again,
            Louder and louder grown;
        Wind of the Kansas plain,
            Rushing a wild cyclone.

Beautiful Kansas town,
　　Smiling 'mid plenty and peace;
　Crowned with the radiant crown
　　Of hope and of joy's surcease.
Music and laughter of radiant youth,
　Mingled with voices of childhood sweet;
Old men seeking the kernel of truth,
　Busily throng on its crowded street.
　　Ceaselessly up and down
　　　Plodding toward the tomb,
　Beautiful Kansas town,
　　Waiting the stroke of doom.

　Bride in her honeymoon,
　　Joy as of mating birds,
　World swinging on in tune —
　　Airs are above all words.
Warm from the rapture of love's embrace,
　Shadow nor cloud-drift darken the way;
Light of love's morn in her upturned face,
　Growing love's growth to the perfect day.
　　Chords that are all in tune,
　　　Filled is their heart's desire,
　Bride in her honeymoon —
　　Love to be tried by fire.

　Sun of a Kansas morn,
　　Shining so clear and bright;
　Smiling on fields of corn,
　　Filling the world with light.
Upward, still rising, he laughs and smiles,
　Smiles on the dust, and the ruins charred;

On the scattered stones and the smoking piles,   ·
   Where the grinning specter of death stands guard.
     Smiles on the hearts forlorn,
       Where man's best hopes are strown;
     Sun of a Kansas morn,
       On the path of the wild cyclone.

· T. S. Brown.

THE OLD SOD SHANTY ON THE CLAIM.

A FRONTIER SONG.

Tune—"*The Little Log Cabin in the Lane.*"

I am looking rather seedy now, while holding down my
    claim,
  And my victuals are not always served the best,
And the mice play slyly round me in my shanty on the
    claim
  As I lay me down alone at night to rest;
Yet I rather like the novelty of living in this way—
  Though my bill-of-fare is always rather tame—
For I'm happy as a clam, on this land of Uncle Sam's,
  In my little old sod shanty on the claim.

CHORUS:

The hinges are of leather, and the windows have no glass,
  While the roof it lets the howling blizzards in;
And I hear the hungry coyote, as he sneaks up thro' the
    grass,
  Round my little old sod shanty on the claim.

THE OLD SOD SHANTY ON THE CLAIM.

But when I left my Eastern home, so happy and so gay,
  To try and win my way to wealth and fame,
I little thought that I'd come down to burning twisted hay
  In my little old sod shanty on the claim.
My clothes are plastered o'er with dough, I'm looking like
    a fright,
  And everything is scattered round the room;
And I fear if P. T. Barnum's man of me should get a sight,
  He would take me from my little cabin home.
          Chorus.

I wish that some kind-hearted miss would pity on me take,
  In this mess, and extricate me from the same:
The angel! how I'd bless her if this her home she'd make,
  In my little old sod shanty on the claim;
And when we'd make our fortunes on the prairies of the
      West,
  Just as happy as two bed-bugs we'd remain;
And we'd forget our trials and our troubles while we'd
    . rest
  In our little old sod shanty on the claim.
          Chorus.

If now and then a little heir to bless our lives was sent,
  Our hearts with honest pride to cheer and flame,
We would surely be content for the years that we had spent
  In our little old sod shanty on the claim;
And after years elapse, and all those little chaps
  To men and honest womanhood have grown,
It won't seem half so lonely if a dozen cozy cots
  Surround our old sod shanty on the claim.
          Chorus.

THE WILD SUNFLOWER.

At early dawn, like soldiers in their places,
    Rank upon rank the golden sunflowers stand ;
Gazing toward the east with eager faces,
    Waiting until their god shall touch the land
To life and glory, longingly they wait,
Those voiceless watchers at the morning's gate.

Dawn's portals tremble silently apart ;
    Far to the east, across the dewy plain,
A glory kindles that in every heart
    Finds answering warmth and kindles there again ;
And rapture beams in every radiant face
Now softly glowing with supernal grace.

And all day long that silent worship lasts,
    And as their god moves grandly down the west,
And every stem a lengthening shadow casts
    Toward the east, ah, then they love him best,
And watch till every lingering ray is gone,
Then slowly turn to greet another dawn.

ALBERT BIGELOW PAINE.

HOW WE TOOK TITUS.
August 16th, 1856.

In the mists of the morning we broke up our camp
    Where the bluff pierced the valley,
And the prairie resounded with rythmical tramp
    Of the Northerners' rally.

For the hunted had turned,—we had suffered too long
    Their rank insolence growing;
Our cup of submission to outrage and wrong
    Had been filled to o'erflowing.

To rob us of ballot, of government — laws
    They had rushed o'er the border,
And now masqueraded as chiefs in the cause,
    Of "law" and of "order."

"For 'Free' State or 'Slave' ye may vote in due time,"
    Was the fair and false promise;
Now, through fraud and through murder, all manner of
    crime,
    They had stolen law from us.

And we said: "While forever we shrink and we yield,
    We grow weaker — not stronger —
If as freemen we'd live, we must now take the field;
    We'll endure it no longer!"

So we whipped them at Franklin, their cannon to gain,
    ("Sacramento," the "talker,")
And on to Fort Saunders, where Hoyt they had slain,
    We had followed Sam Walker.

Where should lightning next strike? red flame blast and
    burn?
        What strongest blow right us?
Th' insulter of freemen must now bide his turn —
        We would take Colonel Titus!

So we broke up our camp, in the mists of the morn,
        ' In the might of our rally;
With no blast of bugle, or sounding of horn,
        We marched out of the valley.

With silence of song-bird the daylight had broke,
        Lacking carol or chorus;
As a child in its sleep Nature smiled, then awoke,
        And the day was before us.

So in silence we press, noting rustle nor stir
        Of scared partridge from cover;
We stay not for shot "on the wing" at the whir
        Of wild grouse or of plover.

We pressed up the slope of the prairie's long swell;
        But our horse had plunged faster,
And charging too madly the stronghold pellmell,
        They had met sore disaster.

Ere the crest of the last ridge we fairly might gain
        We could hear the sharp rattle;
Our comrades were wounded, brave Shombré was slain
        In first onslaught of battle.

Then baffled we paused, looking downward that morn
        On foe safe and undaunted,
Whose solid log walls laughed our bullets to scorn;
        And we raged and we taunted:

"From the shield of your covert you 've slain our true men,
    O chivalrous Titus!
Now, wolf of the prairie, come out from your den,
    Come out, now, and fight us!"

Still sullen and silent as though they 'd ne'er heard,
    The foe kept their cover,
While like bloodhounds in leash, our men chafed for the
    word
    To bid them charge over.

But blue-eyed Sam Walker dashed up on the run,
    Crying "Steady, boys, steady!
'Sacramento' will talk—just unlimber that gun,
    Here 's Tom Bickerton ready!"

And that old Yankee sea-dog, prone to his fun,
    All the time he was sighting,
Grimly pointed his jests as he pointed his gun,
    "Now our wrongs shall have righting!

"Our town beat you down, and our presses you broke—
    Then flung in the river;
Free speech you had stifled through flame and through
    smoke—
    You thought 't was forever!

"For your burnings, in turn, we would fain make it warm
    For your party this morning;
And I 'll send you some type in a different form—
    'Tis the type of your scorning.

"Some fonts for our gun I had gathered of late,
    For I thought you might need 'em;
Here 's the issue upon you of 'Kansas Free State,'
    A new 'Herald of Freedom.'"

Puff! bang! and the issue straightforward went forth
To the thick walls imbedded;
Or scattered their shingles, then plowed up the earth —
For that type was well "leaded"!

Another — that dropped through the roof of their fort
Sending timbers a-flying,
Cries of anguish and fear told the tale of its hurt —
They were wounded or dying.

At the peak of their roof, lo, there flutters a rag!
Is it truce that they tender?
No! — they give up the fight, they fling out a flag,
The white flag of surrender!

A wild, savage shout!   Our boys dash through the door,
With the "Stubbs" in the leading —
"Hoyt!" "Shombré!" their watchwords for vengeance
the more
On their foemen, pale, bleeding.

But Walker, the brave and true-hearted, cries, "Back!
You shall not kill Titus!
They are pris'ners of war whom no man shall attack,
When no longer they fight us."

.   .   .   .

And now on to Lawrence! our morning's work done,
With our captives attendant.   .
Thanks be it to Walker, and Bickerton's gun,
We 're henceforth in ascendant!

Now let the South mourn for a leader o'erthrown!
Lecompte now may rave and for treason indict us!
We have hostage of mark to exchange for their own —
We have got Colonel Titus!

BRINTON W. WOODWARD.

A DREAM OF THE SEA.

A farmer lad in his prairie home
　　Lay 'dreaming of the sea;
He ne'er had seen it, but well he knew
Its pictured image and heavenly hue;
And he dreamed he swept o'er its waters blue,
　　With the winds a-blowing free,
　　With the winds so fresh and free.

He woke! and he said, "The day will come
　　When that shall be truth to me."
But as years swept by him he always found
That his feet were clogged and his hands were bound,
Till at last he lay in a narrow mound,
　　Afar from the sobbing sea,
　　The sorrowing, sobbing sea.

Oh, many there are on the plains to-night
　　That dream of a voyage to be;
And have said in their souls, "The day will come
When my bark shall sweep through the drifts of foam."
But their eyes grow dim and their lips grow dumb,
　　Afar from the tossing sea,
　　The turbulent, tossing sea.

ALBERT BIGELOW PAINE.

.A BORDER MEMORY.

We had moved up to Palmyra,
  In the year of sixty-one,
From our claim on the Neosho
  When our harvesting was done.

Then my husband had enlisted,
  All his heart divinely stirred, ·
And I lived but for the children,
  And to hear the scanty word

That came slowly back to Kansas
  From his precious company,
As the crimson-tide of battle
  Bore it onward to the sea.

Twelve months passed, and the next spring-
     time
  Came with clouds of denser gloom,
And the passion on the prairies
  Broke into more deadly bloom;

And the summer brought the terror
  Close upon the shuddering town,
Of the bloody-handed Quantrell
  On the country sweeping down.

Day by day, the awful menace
  Weighted every lingering hour,
And we slept in troubled dreaming
  Of the fierce marauder's power.

Night by night, I made me ready
    For whatever blow might fall,
With the children all about me,
    Trained to waken at my call.

And I gathered strength and courage
    From the spirit of my son,
Such a bright, intrepid stripling —
    Ne'er a danger he would shun.

He had played so much at soldier,
    Marching ever in the van,
He had taken on the feeling
    And the valor of a man.

So I listened, sad and shrinking,
    When upon a weary day
He came in all flushed and eager,
    With the words he had to say:

"All the men are clean done over,
    Watching so by day and night,
And we boys are going on duty —
    We're just spoiling for a fight.

"But they say there is no danger —
    Quantrell's clear across the line,
And we've but to give the signal
    If we see the slightest sign.

"Jed. and I — for we're the oldest —
    Take our stand at Curran's farm.
You don't care much, do you mother?
    We'll be safe enough from harm."

So I stifled my foreboding,
   Kissed him twice and let him go
Out into the somber twilight,
   In the pride that mothers know.

Such a night! all torn and tortured
   By a host of nameless fears,
I was certain every minute
   There would fall upon my ears

The abrupt determined ringing
   Of the heavy college bell
Which in preconcerted clamor
   Any peril was to tell.

And I seemed to hear the echoes
   Of the warfare far away;
All its horror, doubly dreadful,
   Pressed upon me where I lay.

But at length I slumbered briefly,
   And the dawn in sweet surprise
Filtered through my eastern window,
   Falling gently on my eyes.

Then deploring all my weakness,
   Since no evil chance had come,
I rejoiced in the glad morning
   That would bring my darling home;

So to give him instant welcome
   I flung wide the outer door,—
And I found him 'neath the trellis
   Lying straight upon the floor,

He but slept, I thought in wonder:
 It was death, instead of sleep!
Shot down by a passing ruffian,
 He had still the power to creep

Towards the town so gladly guarded
 In the strength he loved to try,
And but reached the dear home-shelter,
 Spent with effort, there to die.

That same day devoted Lawrence
 Was destroyed by Quantrell's band;
I was only one of many
 Smitten by a murderous hand,

And I tell the story calmly
 Now so many years have passed,
But whoever gives such life-blood
 Feels the anguish to the last.

Yet the sorrow has its glory,
 Shining steady like a star —
All the world had need of Kansas,
 Consecrated by the war.

And the God who guides our battles
 Shaped the purpose of the State;
We have bought her for His uses
 And the price has made us great.

FLORENCE L. SNOW.

KANSAS WEATHER.

When first I came to Kansas State
The day was bright and warm and mellow,
I gamboled o'er the grassy plain
Like any happy, jolly fellow.

The wind was blowing from the south —
A pleasant, gentle, summer breeze,
Flowers were blooming under foot,
And birds sat singing in the trees.

I put my linen duster on;
My pants were thin, my hat was straw;
I loudly praised the Kansas weather,
And thought it best I ever saw.

I then went out to take a ride —
Had hardly ridden half a mile,
The sun shone out so dreadful hot
I nearly roasted for a while.

The sweat dropped from my brow and chin;
I thought I'd seek some cooling shades;
The dust had settled on my face,
Till I was black as ace of spades.

A cloud then hid the shining sun;
The water poured — it did not rain;
By my life, I thought I'd drown,
And never see my home again!

The wind then shifted to the north,
And chilled me to my very bones;
The drops of sweat still on my chin
Were frozen hard as marble stones.

All this happened, as I have said,
In much less than half an hour;
From snow-drifts coming from the north
To rain and shine and blooming flower.

And after this, when e'er I roam,
In winter, summer, spring, or fall,
You'll find I always go prepared
To meet these changes, one and all.

I carry a fan and overcoat,
A linen duster to cover all;
Under my arm you'll always find
A water-proof and umbersoll.

C. S. WHITE.

THE FIELDS OF KANSAS.

Fair is thy brow, O Prairie Queen!
Lovely thy garments, gold and green.

Glory of evening's gates ajar
Rests on thy landscapes stretched afar.

Rests on thy homestead fields that spread
Under the sunset's gold and red.

Pastures green, where the cattle feed
Side by side with the stately steed;

Meadows wide, where the tall, thick grass,
Tosses in billows as swift winds pass;

Fields of clover, all red and sweet,
(Soon to fall at the mower's feet);

Shady groves, in whose cool green breasts,
Farmhouses hide like woodbird's nests; —

All these things do my eyes behold,
Touched and gilded by sunset gold.

All are lovely, yet lovelier still,
On lowland level, on breezy hill —

Fairer at night and fairer at morn,
Are the ripening wheat and the growing corn.

Ripening wheat, it seems to me
A surging, billowy, golden sea.

How it welters and gleams and glows,
Under the sunset's gold and rose.

Use and beauty here meet and greet —
Beautiful, beautiful field of wheat!

Skirting the wheat, to my ear is borne
The rustle of winds in a field of corn.

Serried and ranked, in close array,
Stretching afar, away and away.

Rich and glossy, with streamers green,
Giving in sunshine sheen for sheen,

Giving in moonlight shifting gleams,
Like sparkle of ripples on singing streams ;

Viewed at morning, or viewed at night,
Holdeth the land no fairer sight.

Hoarding the sunshine, drinking the rain ;
Braving the storms that sweep the plain ;

Glistening now, with banners spread,
Under the sunset's gold and red.

Growing, growing, night, noon and morn —
Beautiful, beautiful field of corn !

ELLEN P. ALLERTON.

WHEN THE SUNFLOWERS BLOOM.

I've bin off on a journey ; I jes' got home to-day ;
I traveled east, an' north, an' south, an' every other way ;
I seen a heap of country, an' cities on the boom,
But I want to be in Kansas when the
        Sun-
            Flowers
                Bloom.

You may talk about yer lilies, yer vi'lets and yer roses,
Yer asters, an' yer jassymins an' all the other posies ;
I'll allow they all air beauties an' full 'er sweet perfume,
But there's none of 'em a patchin' to the
        Sun-
            Flower's
                Bloom.

Oh, it's nice among the mount'ins, but I sorter felt shet in;
'T'ud be nice upon the seashore ef it was n't for the din;
While the prairies air so quiet, an' there 's allers lots o'
    room,
Oh, its nicer still in Kansas when the
        Sun-
            Flowers
                Bloom.

When all the sky above is jest ez blue ez blue kin be,
An' the prairies air a wavin' like a yaller driftin' sea,
Oh, it's there my soul goes sailin' an' my heart is on the
    boom,
In the golden fields of Kansas when the
        Sun-
            Flowers
                Bloom.

                    ALBERT BIGELOW PAINE.

A MOUNTAIN INCIDENT.

One bright morning, in the mountains of Colorado, I
stood by my camp-fire watching several companies of cavalry as they rode by from their camp of the night before
at the foot of Cochetopa Pass. Soldiers and commissary
wagons were rapidly winding down the long valley we had
come up the evening before. Two men came out of a
cabin a little way off, where the prohibition law was un-
heard of, and approached my camp. One of them interested me; he was dressed in an outlandish, half-Indian
costume, and looked wild enough, yet when he drew near
and asked permission to light his pipe at my fire he spoke

in such gentle and deferential tones, and with such an unmistakable air of true gallantry, that I felt some woman, somewhere, must feel proud to call him her son.

He bowed gracefully as he bade me good morning; he and his companion returned to the cabin, untied and mounted their horses, and rode down the valley after the troops like a cyclone. They talked loudly, and finally the trembling air bore back faint sounds of terrific Rocky Mountain oaths.

"Who is he?" I asked.

"O, that's Oregon Bill; he is acting as guide for the troops. He is a good-for-nothing drinking brute," replied my driver.

At our noon camp we were overtaken by a young man on horseback, and after the usual greetings were passed, he was asked, "Where did you pass the troops?"

"Down by the widder's," he replied.

"Why, has that woman's husband not got back yet?"

"No, she's alone there yet, with her little children, and all they have to live on is what people give her as they pass. Oregon Bill rode up to her door and gave her a ten-dollar bill and then rode off without saying a word."

I felt justified for my partiality for the dashing stranger; and quietly fancied that sometimes soft angel hands rested in blessing upon his wayward head. I thought that even he might be linked by a beautiful chain of kind and generous deeds to the heart of infinite love; and when the final settlement comes to him — as it will to all — though the protest may be entered, "He was wild and reckless, unconverted; never baptized, either by immersion or sprinkling," I think that a voice, in which the sweetest music of earth and heaven blend, will be heard: "I was hungry, and he gave me meat; thirsty, and he gave me drink; sick at heart, and in the prison of hard circumstances, on the bleak, lonely mountain-side, and he came unto me; the brightness of his kindly deed will guide his footsteps to a higher life. Let Oregon Bill pass."

MRS. S. N. WOOD.

GOVERNOR REEDER'S SPEECH.

"Day by day a crisis approaches us. In after-times posterity will view this as a turning-point — a marked period — such as to us now are the adoption of the Declaration of Independence and the era of the Alien and Sedition laws. We should take each step carefully, so that each shall be a step in the way of progress, and so that no violence be done to the tie that binds the American people together.

"If anyone supposes that any institutions or laws can be imposed by force upon a free and enlightened people, he never knew, or has forgotten, the history of our forefathers. American citizens bear in their breasts too much of the spirit of other and trying days, and have lived too long amid the blessings of liberty, to submit to oppression from any quarter; and the man who, having once been free, can tamely submit to tyranny, is only fit to be a slave.

"I urge the Free-State men of Kansas to forget all minor issues, and pursue with determination the one great object, never swerving, but ever pressing on, as did the wise men who followed the star to the manger, looking back only for fresh encouragement.

"I counsel, first, that peaceful resistance be made to the tyrannical and unjust laws of the spurious Legislature;

that appeal be had to the courts, to the ballot-box, and to Congress for relief from this oppressive load—that violence be deprecated so long as a single hope of peaceable redress remains; and at last, should all peaceful efforts fail, if, in the proper tribunals, there is no hope for our dearest rights, outraged and profaned—if we are still to suffer that corrupt men may reap harvests watered by our tears, then there is one more chance for justice. God has provided, in the eternal frame of things, redress for every wrong, and there still remains to us the steady eye and the strong arm, and we must conquer or mingle the bodies of the oppressors with those of the oppressed upon the soil which the Declaration of Independence no longer protects. I am not apprehensive that such a crisis will ever arrive. I believe that justice may be found far short of so dreadful an extremity, and even should an appeal to arms come, if we are prepared, that moment the victory is won. . . .

"I am reluctant to believe that the correct public sentiment of the South indorses the violent wrongs which have been perpetrated by Missourians upon the people of this Territory, and I wait to hear its rebuke. Should it not come, and all hope of moral influence to correct these evils be cut off, and the tribunals of our country fail us, while our wrongs still continue, what then? Will they have grown easier to bear from long custom? God forbid that any lapse of time should accustom freemen to the duties of slaves, and when such fatal danger as that menaces, then is the time to—

> "'Strike—for your altars and your fires,
> Strike—for the green graves of your sires,
> God, and your native land!'"
> —*Andreas' History.*

THE KANSAS INDIAN'S LAMENT.

Our tribe is less'ning year by year,
    The paleface drives us back—
With us, the bison, bear, and deer
    Before his onward track—
In battle with his arméd power,
The Red Man fears but dares now cower.

The footprints of our moc'sins fade,
    They once left paths for miles,
And the Great Spirit hides in shade,
    No more we see his smiles:
Few wampum belts our tribe needs yet,
For soon the warrior's star will set.

These broad prairies once were ours,
    We fished the many rivers;
On yonder Kaw, embanked with flowers,
    With arrows in our quivers,
With dusky maids, wigwams behind,
We sailed before the singing wind.

The sunflower waved its yellow head,
    Across the grassy plains—
And, like our chieftain, now are dead.
    The spirit herbs for pains:
Paleface, our mild clime 's not for thee,
It moves, with us, toward sundown sea.

Our moons are few, our race is run,
   Some dark fate drags us down;
Less bright the once all-glorious sun,
   The golden stars are brown—
The tall mounds black and dismal loom,
Each day speaks of our coming doom.

Our wasted race,—my father brave,
   My squaw and pappoose too,
All here lie buried in the grave,
   Here rots my swift canoe.

Methinks the paleface might have spared
   Some spot where we 'd abide,—
Spared us, who once owned all, and shared
   With them from tide to tide:
'Tis strange, 'tis passing strange to me,
Why they would drive us in the sea.

Our small tribe 's scattered like the leaves
   And wasted to a few—
Each warrior for the bright past grieves,
   Which vanished from our view!
They wait till Manitou's* voice sounds,
Calling to Happy Hunting Grounds.

We go! the White Race takes our place;
   Great Spirit, what am I!
Once thousands strong, where 's now my race—
   On plains beyond the sky?
O take me too, I would not stay,
When all I loved have passed away!

---

*Great Spirit.

Perchance, when many moons have fled
  And the Great Spirit's wrath,
Our many loved ones, from the dead,
  Will come back to earth's path,
To hunt again the buffalo,
And no pale race to bring us woe.

But soft! methinks I hear a voice?
  Great Manitou's! speaks He!
It makes my craven heart rejoice—-
  O what wouldst Thou with me?
"Be brave! God's Happy Hunting Grounds
Are great and good, and have no bounds!"

                    THOMAS BROWER PEACOCK.

LAWRENCE RAID.

A sound of weeping is in the wind,
  A smell of blood upon the air;
Oh, list to the hoof-beats of a horse,
  And hark to a mother's prayer.
The bunch-grass is redder than the rose,
  The wild bee is flying afar;
While up in the sky a bank of cloud
  Seems trying to put out a star.

An avalanche riding to Lawrence—
  The horse and the rider as one;
The earth seems to quiver with anguish,
  And God holds his breath in the sun;

The eagle of Freedom is wounded,
  And flieth so heavy and low;
While all of the demons of blackness
  Are blowing their trumpets of woe.

The torch was aflame, and the houses
  Were turning to columns of smoke;
The crack of the rifles was knelling
  The pain of sad hearts that were broke.
Then heroes lay down like the rushes,
  So quietly taking their rest;
With red blood the earth became drunken,
  Shed by martyrs asleep on her breast.

That day Death laughed out her shrillest,
  While devils went mad in their glee;
Yet a minor chord in the music
  Was, "Kansas is born to be free."
And Lawrence uprose like the Phœnix,
  No smell of the fire on her gown;
She triumphed, and now is the victor;
  We braid and she weareth a crown.

ELLEN PATTON.

GOLDEN ROD IN KANSAS.

  Again the rains have come,
  And all the earth revives,
  And over fields and prairies
  The golden rod now thrives.

Sweet Kansas golden rod,
What scepters bright you lift,
In every vacant corner,
With growing things adrift.

You herald in our autumn,
And cheerfully essay,
With richest gold our prairies
And our orchards to array.

Oh, hardy little flower !
You speak of courage clear,
And hint to us a lesson
To light life's fading year.

AD. H. GIBSON.

TO A KANSAS REDBIRD.

With coat of brightest flame,
You 're singing in the hedge,
All gray and leafless now ;
Then through the frost-killed sedge,
And through the orchard bare,
From apple tree to peach,
You wing a graceful flight
Some half-hid bough to reach.

There, only partly screened
From watchful human gaze,
You carol forth delightful strains
All through the winter days.

No sweeter bird is there than he
To gladden Kansas homes ;
With scarlet coat and silvery notes,
Our prairies free he roams.

AD. H. GIBSON.

WALLS OF CORN.

Smiling and beautiful, heaven's dome
Bends softly over our prairie home.

But the wide, wide lands that stretched away
Before my eyes in the days of May ;

The rolling prairie's billowy swell,
Breezy upland and timbered dell ;

Stately mansion and hut forlorn —
All are hidden by walls of corn.

All the wide world is narrowed down
To walls of corn, now sere and brown.

What do they hold — these walls of corn,
Whose banners toss in the breeze of morn ?

He who questions may soon be told —
A great state's wealth these walls enfold.

No sentinels guard these walls of corn,
Never is sounded the warder's horn ;

Yet the pillars are hung with gleaming gold,
Left all unbarred, though thieves are bold.

Clothes and food for the toiling poor;
Wealth to heap at the rich man's door;

Meat for the healthy, and balm for him
Who moans and tosses in chamber dim;

Shoes for the barefooted, pearls to twine
In the scented tresses of ladies fine;

Things of use for the lowly cot,
Where (bless the corn) want cometh not;

Luxuries rare for the mansion grand,
Booty for thieves that rob the land; —

All these things, and so many more,
It would fill a book but to name them o'er,

Are hid and held in these walls of corn,
Whose banners toss in the breeze of morn.

Where do they stand, these walls of corn
Whose banners toss in the breeze of morn?

Open the atlas, conned by rule,
In the olden days of the district school.

Point to this rich and bounteous land,
That yields such fruits to the toiler's hand.

"Treeless desert" they called it then,
Haunted by beasts and forsook by men.

Little they knew what wealth untold
Lay hid where the desolate prairies rolled.

Who would have dared, with brush or pen,
As this land is now, to paint it then?

And how would the wise ones have laughed in scorn,
Had prophet foretold these walls of corn,
Whose banners toss in the breeze of morn!

MRS. ELLEN P. ALLERTON.

BEAUTIFUL THINGS.

Beautiful faces are those that wear —
It matters little if dark or fair —
Whole-souled honesty printed there.

Beautiful eyes are those that show,
Like crystal panes where hearth-fires glow,
Beautiful thoughts that burn below.

Beautiful lips are those whose words
Leap from the heart like songs of birds,
Yet whose utterance prudence girds.

Beautiful hands are those that do
Work that is earnest and brave and true,
Moment by moment the long day through.

Beautiful feet are those that go
On kindly ministries to and fro,
Down lowliest ways if God wills it so.

Beautiful shoulders are those that bear
Ceaseless burdens of homely care,
With patient grace and daily prayer.

Beautiful twilight at set of sun,
Beautiful goal with race well won,
Beautiful rest with work well done.

Beautiful graves where grasses creep,
Where brown leaves fall, where drifts lie deep,
Over worn-out hands!   Ah, beautiful sleep.

                                    MRS. ALLERTON.

IN THE EAR, OR IN THE JUG.

Farmer Boggs planted some new seed-corn last spring,
imported from a far-distant land, and as the result gathered two thousand bushels from twenty acres; and he took
a wagon-load to the country town to exchange for some
necessaries of life.

He had just entered the main business street, when a
saloon-keeper hailed him and inquired the price of his corn.

"Forty cents a bushel," said Boggs.

"But I can get plenty of corn for thirty," replied the
dealer in liquid goods.

"Not such corn as this," said the farmer.   "This is a
new kind — grown from imported seed.   Nothing like it
in the State."

"All right," said the saloon-keeper.   "I will take it, as
I have the best family horse in the country, and he shall

have the very best corn in the market; so you may drive around to my barn and throw the corn in the crib, and while there please tell John, my hired man, to give old Faithful a good feed, and have him hitched up by 2 o'clock, for I want to take my wife and two children out riding this afternoon."

Boggs unloaded the corn as directed — got his pay for it, made a few purchases, and left for home — while John promptly at 2 o'clock hitched old Faithful to the phaeton. But as the saloon-keeper, his wife and two little daughters were getting into the vehicle, old Faithful's eyes flashed like fire; he reared up on his hind feet, snorted like a loco-motive, and it was all John could do to hold him. At last, when all were fairly seated, John was told to let him go, and off went old Faithful down the street, wholly unman-ageable, until suddenly turning a corner, over went the phaeton, smashed into splinters, and its occupants sent sprawling into the street.

While the bruised and battered family was being picked up and cared for, a crowd of men succeeded in capturing old Faithful. A veterinary surgeon was called, and as he took hold of the bit, old Faithful's breath struck him fully in the face; he smiled, and said: "There is nothing the matter with the horse, *only he is drunk.*" Drunk on that new kind of corn.

The next day the farmer, ignorant of what had hap-pened, took another load to town; stopped at the saloon, but the proprietor was not in. He then drove around to his residence, rang the bell, and the saloon-keeper, with a patch over one eye, his arm in a sling, nose mashed, hob-bled to the door, and was asked by Boggs if he didn't want to buy another load of corn?

Raising a crutch, he ejaculated: "Corn — corn! do I look as if I needed any more of that kind of corn? Look at my wife there with a broken arm. See my darling little angels bruised beyond recognition. See my three-hundred-dollar phaeton smashed into everlasting smithereens, and old Faithful so humiliated and ashamed that he can't look decent people in the face, and *then* dare to ask *me* if *I* want any more corn; get out of here, you villainous old clodhopper, or I'll set my big dog on you!"

Boggs had two thousand bushels of that kind of corn. He had depended upon it to lift the mortgage off his farm, but now it seemed that all was lost.

He went to a lawyer, and told him his story. The lawyer informed him that all he had to do was to take out a license. A petition was at once prepared and the farmer started out to get signers.

He went first to the saloon-keepers, supposing that they would sign without a word. But he was mistaken.

Instead of signing his petition, they with one accord declared that any man who would sell that kind of corn to be fed to a dumb brute was worse than a heathen.

Even the deacons refused to sign, declaring that they could not stand it to see a colt humiliate and disgrace its mother by reeling through the public streets; or hear a cow bawl at the sight of her besotted calf; while a minister, with a look of indignation that was indescribable, said in thunder tones, that if his party ever licensed the sale of that kind of corn he would never vote its ticket again, and then he quoted Scripture about no drunkard entering the kingdom of God; and, as a final crusher, he asked Boggs what would become of all the poor dumb brutes, if we licensed the sale of that kind of corn. *Then he wept.*

Poor Boggs, discouraged, returned to the office, dropped the petition on the table, sank into a chair as he exclaimed : "Personal liberty is a myth."

The lawyer, moved by sympathy, as lawyers always are, put on his best thinking-cap. In a moment his countenance beamed with joy; he slapped Boggs good-naturedly on the back and said: "Brighten up, old boy, I've got an idea. A capital idea, too; one that lets you out slick and clean, saves your farm, and, above all, preserves your personal liberty. You proceed at once to draw that corn to the distillery, have it made into whisky—and *then* circulate your petition for a license to sell the whisky, and they will all sign it, and thus the dumb brutes will be protected, personal liberty perpetuated, and, besides all that, such a course will not hurt the party. You see it all depends upon whether the corn is sold in a *solid* or *liquid* state."

JOHN P. ST. JOHN.

BLEEDING KANSAS' DAYS.

"Union Soldier" and "Unknown," the marble said,
  An incomplete but perfect story of the dead.
  While little Annie sat upon the mound and played,
  And strewed her flowers upon the sod, her hand was
     stayed;
"What zat say?" asked she, pointing to the modest
    praise.
"It tells," said Uncle Tom, "of Bleeding Kansas' days."

"Oh, tell us," cried the younger Tom, "about the fights,
  And why they fought, and what they did, and all the
     sights."
The old man feebly smiled, and said with honest pride :
"I do not know — there were so many men that died —
  So many wrongs were done — they strove so many
     ways —
'Tis hard to tell the fights of Bleeding Kansas' days.

"And yet we fought them well, and thought we held
     our own,
  And when we lost, a shout went up, and ne'er a moan ;
  We thought we fought for right — we knew we loved
     the cause —
  We shouted, fought and prayed — we had no time to
     pause
  And learn how others strove ; in loyal battle's haze
  We struggled fiercely in those Bleeding Kansas' days.

"They came upon us once to burn the homes we had,
  Came plundering, killing women and their babes —
     thieves mad ;
  We rallied, beat them, caught the leader of the band ;
  He died — the corn grows larger on yon sacred land —
  We could not see our houses burned, and only gaze ;
  We had to kill men in those Bleeding Kansas' days.

"Live those," he said, "who do not love a state thus
     made —
  Whose hearts throb not in anxious hope ?   Can such
     pride fade ?

Who fails in these things could not fight where patriot
    falls ;
Devoid of honor ! such men fill our prisons' walls.
Ah, there were heroes then ; who thinks their faith
    decays ?
Who fight as we fought in those Bleeding Kansas'
    days ? "

His eyes grew dim — no woman's face could sweeter be ;
None moved or spoke, till Annie climbed upon his
    knee ;
She stroked his beard, repeating o'er in plaintive croon,
" What zat say ? " pointing to the words in marble hewn.
" The tale," said he, " of one who died in active praise
Of what we fought to build in Bleeding Kansas' days."

CARL BRANN.

TAKE HEART.

Why court the shadows, friends,
    And grope in gloom and fear ?
Take heart ; look always upward,
    Where the sun is beaming clear.

We were not meant to languish,
    And yield to dark despair ;
The cloudy days are sent
    To make us prize the fair.

AD. H. GIBSON.

THE MODEL OLD COUPLE.

There never was a wedded pair
  That equaled Dad and Mam;
In harvesting he capped the sheaf,
  In spanking she took the palm.

She used to scour the pots and pans,
  While he would scour the hills;
She footed all the stockings,
  And he footed all the bills.

No vices marred his perfect health,
  Or made his eyes grow dim;
The filthy weed that others chewed,
  It was eschewed by him.

He never loafed about the town,
  In wrangle or dispute;
And when he wished to go ahead,
  He often went afoot.

The dumb and helpless beasts of toil
  Received his kindest care;
Of nights he'd shed his cattle, and
  The cattle shed their hair.

He said: "This little rule I find,
  Will win, and seldom lose;
My P's and Q's I always mind,
  And also mind my ewes."

Said he: "Each day I never fail,
  To thank the Lord anew;
He gives to us His rain, and we
  Should give to Him His due."

With love towards her little flock,
  Her heart would overflow;
And when the children needed bread,
  She always kneaded dough.

If any scandal reached her ears,
  While busy with her yarn,
She said she didn't give a snap—
  And then she gave a darn.

Said she: "My neighbors' little sins
  Do not my spirit vex;
In other eyes I see no beam
  If mine are without specs."

Some said her dairy was her god—
  But who our hearts can tell?
If work to worship is akin,
  She loved her cheeses well.

At last, when this contented pair
  Had old and feeble grown,
He sat him down and made his will—
  She had one of her own.

                    Sol. Miller.

A CHURCH-BELL OF MANHATTAN.

[In the spring of 1855 the steamer Hartford arrived at Manhattan, Kansas, with settlers from Cincinnati. On the return voyage she was wrecked and burned near St. Marys. The bell of the steamer was rescued by Judge Pipher, for the Methodist church, and still calls to worship the congregation of the First Methodist Episcopal Church.]

There's a bell that in the steeple
   Of a city church doth hang,
And I hear the waters flowing
   As I listen to its clang.

Once upon a river steamer
   Hung this consecrated bell,
And its iron music mingled
   With the river's sweep and swell.

And that steamer to this city
   Brought the hardy pioneers;
Then adown the shallow river,
   Homeward-bound the vessel steers.

But the boat that has ascended
   Streams for thousand miles or more,
Meets with wreck and conflagration,
   On the Kansas river shore.

Yet the bell somehow was rescued,
   And secured by one who thought
Faith in God, in all beginnings,
   Should profoundly be inwrought.

Years the bell hung in the steeple,
  And companion bell was none;
By its voice to worship calling,
  Who can tell what hearts were won!

Rude no longer is the region,—
  Lies a city in the vale;
And the bells from many steeples
  With their peal the ear assail.

But I listen for the ringing
  Of the old historic bell,
And I hear in its vibrations
  How the waters sweep and swell.

IDA A. AHLBORN.

THE REUNION AT WIDDY MACHREE'S.

Och, Mary, mavourneen, what's this that ye'r tellin'?
  The blue-coated soldiers are coming to-day—
Are drivin' their stakes just furninst of me dwellin'
  To hold a reunion — is that what ye say?

An' me with my rheumatiz kapin me quiet!
  Scarce able to stir from me chair or me bed!
Now over me primises sure they'll run riot,
  And chate ivery eye-tooth jist out of me head.

There's the hins, sure they'll lave of thim niver a feather,
    And me turkeys, as foine ones as iver ye see;
The ducks an' the geese too, they 'll all go togither,
    Och, sorra the day to the Widdy Machree.

There's me garden of cabbages, beets and tomaties,
    That I 've planted an' watered an' tinded so well;
Sure they 'll gather the banes an' they'll dig the peraties,
    An' lave of me onions now niver a shmell.

In me melon patch thrifty the spalpeens will frolic,
    And ate all me cucumbers, groin' so foine;
Could I hear ivery wan of thim shcrame wid the colic,
    I'd niver begrudge thim that fruit of the vine.

Run, Mary, acushla, as fahst as ye 'er able,
    And shut up the pigs in the cellar to shtay;
Put the hins, geese an' turkeys an' ducks in the shtable,
    And lock the door, darlint, an' bring me the kay.

Do n't stop now, for whisht! yes, I hear thim a comin'!
    There's the fife an' the bugle — Och, wirra the day!
Sure my heart's batin fahst at the sound of the drummin'
    That brings back the time whin me Pat wint away.

Whin he wore the blue coat, wid the buttons and trimmin'
    And carried the flag wid an Irishman's joy —
Oh, the ould times come back, an' me eyes are a dimmin'
    Whin I look at the sojers an' think of me boy.

See! they 're marchin' in now, wid the drum still a batin':
    An' was I begrudgin' me banes an' all that,
An' the trifle of mate that the boys wad be atin',
    Who followed the ould flag along wid me Pat?

An' me turkeys an' hins, was I tryin' to hide thim?
　An' countin' the likes of a pratie or egg,
To the boys wid the empty sleeve hangin' beside thim,
　Or hobblin' about on a stump of a leg?

Bad luck to me now for a stingy ould hathen!
　Go, open the doors an' set ivery thing free;
An'—but here comes the captin—I'm wantin' to say
　　t'him,
　"The top of the mornin' from Widdy Machree.

"There's the fruit an' the fowls an' the bit of a garden;
　There's the foine pigs for roastin'; and now, do ye mind,
Niver shtop to be axin' me lave or me pardon,
　But take all ye want—take the best you can find.

"Take freely an' welcome, thin wad you remember,
　An' ould Irish comrade, bould, gallant, an' true,
Who fell at Antietam wan day in September,
　While houldin' the banner an' wearin the blue."

MAGGIE MACKILMER.

KANSAS.

What time the clouds of Liberty's duress
Hung darkly o'er its mighty wilderness,

Then fled in storm, leaving a wondrous light
Like morn of splendor flashed from rayless night,

Under the lullaby of waving grass
What powers slept, what life, what loveliness!

O'er the wide grave divinest incense blew
As flower goblets spilled their perfumed dew;

And sacrament was in the mystic spell
Of solitude rife with the invisible.

Silence sublime! poetic mood of earth
Ere flower roots turn gems of human worth.

But list, wild roses! hear the rushing wing
That fans to life more glorious blossoming!

The purple seas, presto! were green and gold
As magic like the billowy map unrolled;

The starry pendulum of destiny
Swung wide, driven by the winds of Liberty.

For Freedom's angel 'twas whose tempest sweep
Awaked the prairies from their deathful sleep,

And o'er their portals crossed the shining words,
"Virtue, courage, culture," as sentry swords.

And now, the fantasies of Freedom's thought
On nature's page in forms and colors wrought,

Mirror in the blue depths of matchless skies
The shadow of an earthly paradise;

And fix upon our country's flag a star,
Like Venus shines in peace, like Mars in war.

A. A. B. CAVANESS.

JAMES MONTGOMERY.

Montgomery, thy manly shade
   Now rests in peace.   The sacred grove
   Now decorates thy grave in love;
   And weeping waters gurgling move
Close to thy feet where thou art laid.

Thy watchful eyes and daring hand
   Guarded the way for Liberty —
   Here at the gates of Linn we see
   Thy stalwart blade and standard high,
As thou a sentinel didst stand!

Sweet be thy rest!   And while the years
   Roll round, thy name in memory green
   Shall live, and here each year be seen
   Thy comrades come, and o'er thee lean,
And drop the tribute of their tears.
            — From "Song of Kansas."

SELECTIONS FROM "TWO PICTURES; A CEN-TENNIAL POEM."

Wedded to Freedom on her hundredth birthday!
   Mature in years, and life aglow with health,
Bright buds of hope are blooming on her pathway,
   Prophetic promise of her future wealth!
Her home — a continent of God's creating,
   Her dower — primeval nature's boundless store

Of soil productive, and rich mines awaiting
  To lay their buried treasures at her door.
Her pride—the mem'ry of the noble martyrs,
  Whose blood baptized the realm of liberty.
Her strength—a serried host of sons and daughters
  Whose hearts and arms are nerved by loyalty.
Her glory—freedom of the humblest person
  Who breathes unfettered from the taint of crime.
Her power—the written law, blest Freedom's charter,
  That guards her people's rights in every clime.
Her shrine—the sanctuary of myriad hearthstones,
  Whence prayer or praise ascends.   Her faith the creed
That God vouchsafes to every soul created,
  Such free oblation as it choose or need.
Her wealth—the wisdom of an age supernal.
  Her hope—the genius of the good and true.
Her flag—a symbol of the stars eternal,
  That deck the vaulted dome of heaven's blue!
Her trust—the keeping of the truth immortal
  That Right and Justice, with their chastening rod,
Are guardian angels of the waiting portal
  That opens upward to the throne of God!
Our mother! be thy future destiny
  To wield the scepter of a world made free!

J. LEE KNIGHT.
(In Frost's Collection.)

JULY FOURTH.

To-day the light is clearer,
And brings the shadow nearer
Of a planet yet to whirl the circle of the sun ;
It is a horoscope
Casting the human hope,
Subtle with meaning deep of what the world has won.

The grandest march of soul
Toward the noblest goal,
Was when our glorious fathers marched to July Fourth,
And set in this day's light
The truth of the Infinite
That all mankind are brothers, and of equal worth.

The grandest march of heart
Was when the human mart
Was burned to ashes in the deathless July flame.
And a blazing sword is set
Athwart the bayonet
Upon the crimson line we crossed from deathless
shame.

O day of liberty ;
Your light is destiny !
Your force and thunder pallid monarchs feel and hear ;
You beamed at Lexington,
And Appomattox won,
And now your crystals fall upon a hemisphere.

Your stars of hope unfurled
Shine to the nether world,
And take the breath of heaven with their matchless
gleam ;
And all that is to be
Upon the land and sea
Glows in the radiance of your prophetic beam.

For swift the shadow flies
Of a planet in the skies ;
The sun shall kiss from Aries and Capricorn ;
Earth shall be born again,
And peace, good-will to men,
Are in the bugles sweet of this transcendent morn.

A. A. B. CAVANESS.

THE INTERREGNUM.

Us fellers hev a hundred ways
To tell the seasons by ;
Not countin' in the kind of days
Ner culler of the sky,
Fer them is purty badly mixt,
An' jes es like es not,
'At when you git yerself all fixt
Fer it to be right hot,
The wind 'll kinder sidle 'round
An' give a sudden whoo,
An' set yer teeth to shakin', an'
Yer hands to gettin' blue ;

But if they 's eny wether 'at
   You can 't depend on 't all,   .
It 's when the Kansas summer is
   A turnin' into fall.

They 's no use much to write it down
   An' stowe it 'way in books :
Next year perhaps 't 'll change aroun',
   In all exceptin' looks
Of trees an' grass an' sich like things.
   They 's jes one way to tell,
An' that 's to watch what each year brings
   An' stay here quite a spell,
An' when you see the yeller 's
   All blowed off the sunflower's head,
An' the orn'ry little fellers
   Fightin' with 'em now they 're dead ; .
An' when you see the blue smoke hang
   'Round woods an' hills an' all,
You bet the Kansas summer is
   A turnin' into fall.

 · An' when yu're loafin' 'round the crick
   Down by the swimmin' hole,
The lonesomeness jest makes you sick,
   Fer not a single soul,
Is in to wet the ol' spring-board,
   'At seems so warped an' dry ;
The slidin'-down place too is rough
   By cattle passin' by.
So when you git to town agin,
   They hain't a bit of harm

In stoppin' where the sun hez bin,
   (The sidewalks is so warm,)
To rest yer tired foot 'at 's got
   A sticker in the ball : —
All these 're signs 'at summer is
   A turnin' into fall.

An' when we have to wear our shoes,
   The mornins 're so cool ;
An' when we get a good excuse
   To take 'em off at school,
At recess to play "three-ol'-cat,"
   Er "scrub," er "pull-away,"
Er eny other games like that
   Which all us fellers play —
It feels jest like the spring wuz here
   To be barefoot again ;
But though our feet seem cold an' queer
   When school is taken in,
With all the girls a snick 'rn' ez
   We stand 'long side the wall,
Us boys can recomember then,
   'At summer's turn'd t' fall.   ·

                              WILL A. WHITE.

THE ATHENA OF AMERICAN STATES.

Kansas is the Athena of American States. Thirty-six years ago the Slave Oligarchy ruled this country. Fearing that the birth of new States in the West would rob it of supremacy, the Slave Power swallowed the Missouri Compromise, which had dedicated the Northwest to Freedom. The industrious North, aroused and indignant, struck quick and hard, and Kansas, full-armed, shouting the war-cry of Liberty, and nerved with invincible courage, sprang into the Union. She at once assumed a high place among the States. She was the deadly enemy of Slavery; she gave voice and potency to the demand for its abolition; and she aided in burying secession in its unhonored grave. The war over, she became the patron, as she had been during its continuance the exemplar, of heroism, and a hundred thousand soldiers of the Union found homes within the shelter of her embracing arms. The agriculturist and the mechanic were charmed by her ample resources and inspired by her eager enterprise. Education found in her a generous patron, and to literature, art and science she has been a steadfast friend. Her pure atmosphere invigorated all. A desert disfigured the map of the continent, and she covered it with fields of golden wheat and tasseling corn.

She has extended to women the protection of generous laws and enlarged opportunities for usefulness.

In war she was valiant and indomitable, and in peace she has been intelligent, energetic, progressive and enterprising. The modern Athena, type of the great Greek goddess, is our Kansas.

JOHN A. MARTIN.

OPPORTUNITY.

Maker of human destinies am I!
    Fame, love and fortune on my footsteps wait.
.   Cities and fields I walk; I penetrate
Deserts and seas remote, and passing by
    Hovel and mart and palace, soon or late
    I knock unbidden once at every gate!
If sleeping, wake; if feasting, rise before
    I turn away.   It is the hour of fate,
    And they who follow me reach every state
Mortals desire, and conquer every foe
    Save death; but those who doubt or hesitate,
    Condemned to failure, penury and woe,
Seek me in vain and uselessly implore;
    I answer not, and I return no more.

                                JOHN J. INGALLS.

KANSAS: 1874–1884.

1874—PER ASPERA.

Cheerless prairie stretching southward,
    Barren prairies stretching north;
Not a green herb, fresh and sturdy,
    From the hard earth springing forth.
Every tree bereft of foliage,
    Every shrub devoid of life,
And the two great ills seemed blighting
    All things in their wasting strife.

As the human heart, in anguish,
   Sinks beneath the stroke of fate,
So at last, despairing, weary,
   Bowed the great heart of our State.
She had seen her corn-blades wither
   'Neath the hot wind's scorching breath;
She had seen the wheat-heads bending
   To the sting of cruel death.

She had·seen the plague descending
   Thro' the darkened, stifling air,
And she bent her head in sorrow,
   Breathing forth a fervent prayer.
And the fierce winds, growing fiercer,
   Kissed to brown her forehead fair,
While the sun shone down unpitying
   On the brownness of her hair.

Then she looked into the future,
   Saw the winter, ruthless, bold,
Bringing her disheartened people
   Only hunger, want and cold.
Looking, saw her barefoot children
   Walk where snow-sprites shrink to tread;
Listening, heard their child-lips utter
   Childish prayers for daily bread.

Low she bowed her head, still thinking
   O'er her people's woes and weal,
And the ones anear her only
   Heard the words of her appeal.

Send that faint cry onward, outward,
Swift as wire wings can bear,
"Sisters, help me or I perish —
Heaven pity my despair!"

1884 — AD ASTRA.

Verdant wheat-fields stretching southward,
Fruitful orchards east and west;
Not a spot in all the prairie
That the spring-time has not blessed.
Every field a smiling promise,
Every home an Eden fair,
And the angels, Peace and Plenty,
Strewing blessings everywhere.

As the heart of nature quivers
At the touch of spring-time fair,
So along the State's wide being
Thrilled the answer to her prayer.
She has seen her dauntless people
Ten times turn and sow the soil;
She has seen the same earth answer
Ten times to their faithful toil.

She has felt the ripe fruit falling
In her lap from bended limbs;
She has heard her happy children
Shouting their thanksgiving hymns.
She has seen ten golden harvests;
Now, with grateful joy complete,
She has poured the tenth, a guerdon,
At her benefactor's feet.

Thou canst not forget, O Kansas,
　　All thine own despair and woe;
Who hath long and keenly suffered
　　Can the tenderest pity show.
Not in vain the needy calleth —
　　Charity her own repays,
And thy bread, cast on the waters,
　　Will return ere many days.

Peace, thine angel, pointeth upward,
　　Where the gray clouds break away;
And athwart the azure heavens
　　Shineth forth Hope's placid ray.
Look to Heaven and to the future —
　　Grieve no longer o'er the past;
Through thy trials, God bless thee, Kansas —
　　See, the stars appear at last.

HATTIE HORNER.

THE STORY OF THE FLAG.

There is a subtle passion within each human heart
That sets the pulse to throbbing, and makes each fiber start;
That stirs the soul to frenzy in battle's stern array,
Or cheers the weary traveler in countries far away;
That prompts each human being with heart and voice to cry:
"All hail thee! glorious banner, mount upward to the sky,"
Wherever fate may find him, whenever he beholds
His country's banner hoisted, and the breeze caress its folds.

But why the Turkish people, crushed 'neath the Sultan's
    heel,
Or why the people of the Czar, who to that despot kneel,
Should feel the same emotion as the people of a land
Whose banner stands for liberty, we do not understand.
And yet the Turk will rally 'round the crescent and the star,
The Russian people gather 'neath the eagles of the Czar;
And each will fight as bravely, and each as loudly cry:
"All hail our glorious banner! mount upward to the sky,"
As if their waving banners were bulwarks of the free,
Upheld by Freedom's goddess that all the world might see.

If they, with such devotion, 'round such a flag will stand,
O children of Columbia, who occupy a land
Where in each freeman's ballot, and in each starry fold
Of that banner floating o'er us, is a story that is told
To the men of every nation; to the men of every clime;
And is carved in burnished letters on the Pantheon of Time,
Of how our noble sires once in Freedom's holy name,
Did trample on the despot's rule and rend the tyrant's
    chain.

And then to make a banner that would represent their deeds;
That would stand for perfect freedom to all people, and all
    creeds,
They took their bloody foot-prints, left on the driven snow,
And made those stripes of red and white that set our hearts
    aglow;
Then, reaching upwards took the stars, their freedom to
    imply,
And placed them on a back-ground with the azure of the
    sky.

Shall we, whose banner represents the brotherhood of man,
Be any less heroic than the tyrant's servile clan;
Whose highest sense of duty, to country or to flag,
Is bowing down in rev'rence, and evermore to drag
The chains of despotism which bind their spirits down;
To regulate their actions by the tyrant's smile or frown?

No, hoist that flag forever o'er the rampart of your hearts.
Humanity will bless it for the lesson it imparts.
It makes the despot tremble as it flutters in the gale;
He fears that gentle flutter far above his people's wail.
And as the weary sailor, while many leagues from shore,
Is cheered by fragrant breezes that have gently wafted o'er
Some far-off fertile island, with its groves of spice and palm,
And in passing thus were laden with the perfume of its
    balm;
So the down-trodden people, of every land and clime,
With gladdened hearts are turning to this flag of source
    divine.
They breathe in every zephyr that has kissed its starry fold
The spirit of our sires who that banner did uphold.

O children of Columbia! each acting well his part,
Will wear that banner graven on the tablet of his heart:
Will speed the message onward, o'er all the land and sea,
"The stars and stripes are waving for all humanity";
Will shout, "Wave on, Old Glory! Thy stars and stripes
    shall float·
O'er peaceful school-bell music, or warlike bugle's note";
Will feel his pulses throbbing to the music of the drum,
No more, than when in times of peace, his duty whispers,
    "Come."
                   EDWARD T. BARBER.

EARLY REMINISCENCES.

Two weeks before the first party of the New England Emigrant Aid Company arrived in Kansas, a little band of Ohio emigrants toiled up the hill and rested on the very spot where now stands that noble building, the Kansas State University. The two-hours rest on that hill will never be forgotten. It was the last Sabbath in July, 1854. How vast the country seemed to that lonely little party! As far as the eye could reach the scene was unbroken by the work of human hands. The quiet, good-natured oxen, standing patiently in the shadow of the high covered wagon, seemed like part of the family.

The party passed on, and pitched their tent four miles further west, on the California road.

Thus commenced that queer, half-civilized way of living, a home without a house. I remember what an effort mother made to keep in sight the old landmarks, and dear old home ways. The family altar was established, the blessing asked at the table, an extra plate laid for the stranger. Often was our camp-fire a beacon-light to the benighted traveler.

Our tent was pitched near a spring. Father made a comfortable shade of green boughs over the door of our tent. Other tents were soon set up near us, until we had quite a cheery little settlement.

The weather was hot and dry; the spring failed, and we suffered for good water.

One Saturday noon a violent storm came up; fortunately for us, father was at home. The other men were away looking for claims, or hunting. The storm came on in such awful grandeur, such magnificent fury, as we had never witnessed before. The thunder rolled and crashed over us. The rain poured down in torrents. The wind blew as if it would sweep the prairie clean. It required the united efforts of the family to hold the tent in place.

After the violence of the storm had passed it remained cloudy and threatening, and turned cold. Our neighbors returned to their fallen homes. The night came on early and dark. Everything was soaking-wet and cold—no fire, no supper—not even a place to sit down. Father was equal to the emergency. How he did it I never knew, but he soon had a blazing fire under the cover of boughs that had nobly withstood the storm. As the bright, cheerful fire lighted up the prairie, father called out to our neighbors to come. They waited for no second invitation, for they were wet, cold, and hungry.

Now was mother's opportunity to show that she too was equal to the emergency. With true housewifely care she protected her bread, which was ready to bake when the storm came upon us. By the use of soda she soon had good light biscuit, which Mrs. S. N. Wood baked in a Dutch oven, while mother made a boilerful of coffee, and everyone was served with hot coffee and bread—nothing else, but it was a feast.

The dark night; the threatening clouds overhead; the blazing wood-fire casting a weird light far out over the tall prairie grass, still dripping with the rain; around and near the fire, seated on logs and benches, a little company of men fresh from comfortable New England homes, unused to anything like "roughing it."

The night was spent by the fire.

The next morning the sun rose in all his regal splendor,

as if to repair the damage done by the storm. Tents were set up, beds, blankets and clothing were spread out to dry. Soon all things were in comfortable order again.

Soon the cabin was built and we moved into it. It was without floor, doors, or windows. As it was called the best house on the road, we could not complain. By the 10th of August a flourishing city of tents had sprung up as if by magic, and was called New Boston, Yankee-town, and Thayer. It was finally named Lawrence, in honor of Amos A. Lawrence, of Boston.

Mrs. Sarah Lyons Pinkston.

KANSAS.

Tune, "*Gospel Bells.*"

What magic wand or wizard
   Touched the desert, barren, wide,
Changed it to a land of plenty,
   Walled with corn — the good State's pride?
What wonder is this thing!
   Not a land of barren years —
Kansas — land of orchards, harvests,
   Menaced not by famine-fears.

CHORUS:

Thrice redeemed, Freedom's land,
   Prosper all thy causes great!
Hail thee, State! Bravely stand!
   Long live our noble State!

Declared it was of olden
    That the weak should lead the strong.
So did Kansas, Anti-Slavery,
    Lead against great Slavery's wrong.
The angel saw, and passed
    Unavenged the nation's door;
There was blood upon the lintel —
    Kansas martyr-blood it bore.

                    Chorus.

The State that once in conflict
    Gained a broken slave-chain link,
Once more leads the nation's forces
    'Gainst the slavery of drink.
Arise, O State, and make
    This, thy latest triumph, sure —
Thou that ever hast done battle
    For the good, the true, the pure!

                    Chorus.

We sing thy praises, Kansas,
    Upon this thy natal day,
Sing the song of thy glad triumph
    Over long and toilsome way.
Great Kansas commonwealth,
    Thrown upon the grassy plain,
Rich with richest good of statehood,
    May thy gleaned stars never wane.

                    Chorus.

                        Mary Ray McIntire.

KANSAS—ITS PAST, PRESENT, AND FUTURE.

Recorded—read on history's brightest page—
Written in blood, a story ne'er forgot,
Of days agone; when pioneers endured
Privations, hardships, on this sacred spot.
We read of all the unforgotten past,
That o'er the present its reflections cast,
And hearts then fired with patriotic zeal,
Yet live, nor time shall their brave deeds conceal.

The present, can we need to tell in rhyme
Of this, our glorious age, the present time?
To-day stands forth, unparalleled and grand,
And Kansas leads the van, in our vast land.
The heroes of the past we still revere;
Their spirits, "marching on," are reverenced here;
And as the present, teeming with its light,
Yields us its bounties, all seems glad and bright.

And in the future, glorious, grand, sublime,
None may foretell the change of coming time,
But this we know: The hand that in the past
Crowned us with peace and blessings rich and vast,
Shall guide, uphold, our mighty State alway;
And Kansas hold her rank in fame to-day.
First in our hearts, our State shall always be,
Home of the brave, the birthplace of the free.

LAURA E. NEWELL.

THE NATAL HOUR.

Decorate the Thirtieth of May!
  · Shall we now the great act deplore
    Which gave us Kansas? Nevermore.
    She was called fresh from the dark shore
Of time; she came; hail, mighty day!

All hail! Kansas this day was born;
    Not full fledged and armed, like fair
    Minerva from the matted hair
    Of Jove, to wing her flight in air,
And chant *Ad astra* to the morn.

But in the dark and sullen storm
    Of civil strife; like one without
    A friend or home; and tossed about
    Forlorn, and mocked by the rude shout
Of ruffian bands in demon's form.

Sweet Kansas of the fragrant plain!
    Thy natal hour shall mark a day
    Wreathed in flowery love; whose bright ray
    Shall gild the world, and whose sweet lay
Shall charm like some Æolian strain.

        —From Joel Moody's "Song of Kansas."

THE HOME.

No spot so dear on earth as home.
 We build the home; this builds the State.
 This, loyal, makes the nation great—
 And all from love. No hand of fate
Builds or pulls down a nation's dome.

No happy footsteps from the home
 E'er trod the path which treason takes.
 No hand from happy fireside shakes
 The murderer's blade, nor it forsakes
To Cæsar kill, or rule great Rome.

Kansas, in this thy glories rise—
 In this thy strength. Thy people here
 Their plain and humble structures rear—
 They plow and plant at home, nor fear
That there an execution lies.

'Tis sweet to know that here the State
 Protects the home—that she has thrown
 Around the hearth and wife her own
 Strong arm—that this no kingly crown
Could do, nor more on grandeur wait.

Nor shall the curse of drink, *strong drink*,
 Whose pain is as the adder's sting,
 Sure, quick, and deadly, ever bring
 To Kansas home its guilt, and fling
The household gods on ruin's brink.

This has made Kansas great — to this
    She owes her growth, her power and wealth;
    Her brawny arm and sturdy health;
    She gains by prowess, not by stealth,
And *home* brings all her victories.
            —*From Joel Moody's "Song of Kansas."*

"AD ASTRA PER ASPERA."

"Ad Astra per Aspera "—
    Through difficulties to the stars,
Our State has grandly weathered storms;
    No cloud its peaceful sky now mars,
    No conflicts rage, no grievous wars :
    Through difficulties to the stars.

No fugitive upon our soil,
    As in the past for refuge came,
But all men free; God's noblemen.
    For black and white are His the same,
    A brotherhood — His sacred tie,
    Our God hath given victory.

As long as suns shall rise and set,
    As long as stars shall brightly shine,
    Our Kansas shall be known afar.
    Fairest of States, what fame is thine,
    What records histories unfold,
    Yet not the half has e'er been told.

Ad Astra per Aspera —
All honor to thy heroes brave;
In loyal hearts they still shall live,
Who burst the fetters of the slave.
On history's page their names shall glow,
While suns shall gleam and waters flow.

Then for God's blessing, and his smile
For all His mercies kindly sent,
To heaven let our prayers ascend,
Until earth's days have all been spent,
To God, the glory and the praise,
The author of these golden days.

LAURA E. NEWELL.

KANSAS.

My home is in Kansas, that fearless young State,
    'Mid wide prairie lands of the West:
We have tried many kinds of temperance laws,
    And think Prohibition the best.

We like Prohibition because it can say
    To the man who is selling strong drink:
" You are breaking the law, and your dram-shop must
        close " —
A very good doctrine, we think.

If instead of this law, we licensed saloons
    With a license low, middle, or high,
We could only look on while they kept open doors,
    And say as we sadly pass by:

"Sell on, and grow rich while your patrons grow poor,
  Ruin manhood and boyhood so fair ;
Our license permits you to sell, while we take
  Of your money and crime our full share."

No ! no ! here in Kansas we 'll never say that,
  But prove with each on-coming year,
That the law which prohibits is best, since we find
  'Tis the only one liquor-men fear.

[*Anonymous.*]

THE OLD SOLDIER.

[NOTE. — From George R. Peck's address delivered to the old soldiers at the Home at Leavenworth, Kansas.]

"The old soldier grows tired as the years increase, and he hears only in dreams the roll of drums and the noise of battle. He loves his ease in the quiet afternoon, and feels, as he did not once, how sweet are the ministrations of sleep. Death need not come to seek him, for, half-way up the slope the veteran is marching, if not so gaily as in old days, still resolutely and bravely as becomes one who is not afraid to meet whatever foe may come. And lo ! Death carries neither lance nor spear ; but only the welcome emblem of white which is the sign of everlasting truce. It must be sweet to know that the battle is over forever ; it must be pleasant to sleep in the mercy of Him who hath made it the 'balm of hurt minds.' Let us be patient. To them the hour will come, and the repose that awaits the resurrection and the life."

THE SUNFLOWER OF KANSAS.

A flower for the nation !   What shall the blossom be?
A blossom rare, to shine in air, on land and on the sea,
To lead the van of armies like the sign the Romans bore,
And o'er the brave on the heaving wave, speed alway to
    the fore.

A flower for the nation !   What shall the blossom be?
The rose, the laurel, the princely fleur de lis ?
The May-flower of the pilgrims, or the violet royal blue,
The golden rod, the daisy, good, and fair, and true?

Aye, a flower for the nation !   That follows still the light ;
With heart of gold that ne'er grows old, and fate that's
    ever bright ;
That to the wildest breezes tosses loftily its crest,
Choose what ye will, but give to us the sunflower of the
    West.
                                  [*Anonymous.*]

THE REPORTER AND THE TRAVELING MAN.
(Adapted from Kansas Chief.)
DRAMATIS PERSONÆ: *A drummer with his grip ; a reporter with his note-book.*

Reporter : "How's wheat in southern Kansas? "

Drummer : "Wheat !   You never saw the like !   The farmers down in southern Kansas had to rent the public roads to get room to stack their wheat.   Wasn't room enough in the fields to hold the stacks.   I saw one —"

R. "How is the fruit crop? "

D. "Fruit! You never saw the like! Apples as big as cannon-balls, growing in clusters as big as hay-stacks. I saw one apple that—"

R. "Do n't the trees break down?"

D. "Trees! You never saw the like! The farmers planted sorghum in the orchards, and the stalks grew up like telegraph poles and supported the limbs. I saw one stalk of sorghum that was two feet—"

R. "How is the broom-corn crop?"

D. "Broom-corn! You never saw the like! There has n't been a cloudy day in southern Kansas for a month. Can't cloud up. The broom-corn grew so high that it kept the clouds swept off the face of the sky as clean as a floor. They will have to cut the corn down if it gets too dry. Some of the broom-corn stalks are so high that—"

R. "How is the corn crop?"

D. "Corn! You never saw the like! Down in the Neosho and Fall river and Arkansas bottoms the corn is as high as a house. They use step-ladders to gather the roasting-ears!"

R. "Are n't step-ladders pretty expensive?"

D. "Expensive! Well, I should say so; but that is n't the worst of it. The trouble is, the children climb up into the corn-stalks to hunt eagles' nests, and sometimes fall out and kill themselves. Four funerals in one county last week from that cause. I attended all of them. That is why I am so sad. And mind you, the corn is not more than half grown. A man at Arkansas City has invented a machine which he calls the Solar Corn Harvester and Child Protector. It is inflated with gas like a balloon, and floats over the corn-tops, and the occupants reach down and cut off the ears with a cavalry saber. Every Kansas farmer has a cavalry saber, and — "

R. "Do they make much cider in Kansas?"

D. "Cider! You never saw the like! Oceans of it. Most of the Cowley county farmers have filled their cisterns with cider. A proposition was made a few days ago to the Water Works Company of Arkansas City to supply the town with cider through the mains, but the company were compelled to decline because they were afraid the cider would rust the pumps. They were sorry, but they said they would have to continue to furnish water, although it cost more. I saw one farmer who — "

R. "How is the potato crop?"

D. "Potatoes! You never saw the like! I know men in the Arkansas valley who were too poor last year at this time to flag a bread wagon, and now they have pie three times a day. One fellow that — "

(Exit reporter during the delivery of this sentence, as if having urgent business elsewhere.)

THE HOMES OF KANSAS.

The cabin homes of Kansas!
    How modestly they stood,
Along the sunny hillsides,
    Or nestled in the wood.
They sheltered men and women,
    Brave-hearted pioneers;
Each one became a landmark
    Of Freedom's trial years.

The sod-built homes of Kansas!
  Though built of Mother Earth,
Within their walls so humble
  Are souls of sterling worth,
Though poverty and struggle
  May be the builder's lot.
The sod-house is a castle
  Where failure enters not.

The dugout homes of Kansas!
  The lowliest of all,
They hold the homestead title
  As firm as marble hall.
Those dwellers in the cavern,
  Beneath the storms and snows,
Shall make the desert places
  To blossom as the rose.

The splendid homes of Kansas!
  How proudly now they stand
Amid the fields and orchards,
  All o'er the smiling land.
They rose up where the cabins
  Once marked the virgin soil,
And are the fitting emblems
  Of patient years of toil.

God bless the homes of Kansas!
  From poorest to the best;
The cabin of the border,
  The sod-house of the west;

> The dugout, low and lonely,
>   The mansion, grand and great;
>   The hands that laid their hearthstones
>   Have built a mighty State.

Sol. Miller.

SOL. MILLER AS A POET.

Kansas people are emotional. They feel all the pleasure
and all the pain — in poetic pains — for nearly every Kansan writes poetry. The Kansas writers are not all imita-
tors, either. Dialect poetry was written in Kansas before
J. Whitcomb Riley quit sign-painting.

Sol. Miller, editor of the Troy *Chief*, was the first poet
to reach the State of Kansas. A great many of his early
poems were political hits, and lost force after a campaign.
In 1860 he wrote his "Invocation to the Ground Hog."
He always observes the day. His humor is broad, his
rhyme of the homely kind. He admires Hood enough to
write somewhat like him. He loves to write poetry, but
hides his work. If he prints a poem he does not claim it.
For this reason few people have found him out. He would
not put his things in book form if the cost were paid by
friends. He has some vanity — all men have, if women
haven't — but his is wrapped up somewhere. As he seldom leaves home it may be in his dingy office, or more
probably in his excellent newspaper. He has a most
remarkable memory. He reads his exchanges so closely
that he knows all about people he has never seen. He is
strong, brave, honest. He hurts people often — but with
the stern, old-fashioned weapon of truth.

Of his poems he likes "Pawpaws Ripe" best.

One poem is much liked by the newspapers, and as the birthday of the State nears, year after year, they print it. He calls it the "Homes of Kansas," and first speaks of the modest cabin, the sod-built homes, the dugout homes, the lowliest of them all; then he refers to the splendid homes of Kansas.

As the ear is pitched, the mind is pleased. Sol. Miller is the poet of plain people. He has not made the babbling brook tumble down in print; he has not tamed the wild, untrained note of the bird. The old willows that so idly stand on mossy banks and flirt with the river that flows on forever, have not been disturbed by him; but he has recalled sweetly pure memories, and given us again and again the perfume of flowers that faded long ago; he has given us sentiment that has softened the hard lines of real life and made brighter the plain working-day.

Ewing Herbert.

THE TEACHER.

"How shall we add to earthly beauty?"
    An angel asked one day.
"By teaching man it is his duty
    To smooth his neighbor's way.

"To teach mankind the art of living
    Is doing heaven's will;
It would be well if more were giving
    To that their time and skill.

"'Tis true, if judged by earthly measure,
  They toil for little pay,
And very few their hours of leisure,
  If faithful on the way.

"When conscious that they know their mission,
  And do their labor right,
It gives to life a rich fruition
  And makes the dark seem light."

The angel smiled, and said with laughter:
"I'm going with a crown."
A host of angels started after,
  And quickly followed down.

They placed the crown, with richest blessing,
  Upon the teacher's brow;
If she is onward, upward pressing,
  She wears it, even now.

                              B. W. ALLSWORTH.

ON THE FARM.

How sweet to lean on Nature's arm,
And jog through life upon the farm;
Merchants and brokers spread a dash
A little while, then go to smash;
But we can keep from day to day,
The even tenor of our way.
(There go those horses! Quick, John! catch
    'em —
They 'll break their necks! You did n't hitch
    'em.)

How sweet and shrill the plow-boy's song,
As merrily he jogs along;
The playful breeze about him whirls,
And tosses wide his yellow curls.
His hands are brown, his cheeks are red —
An ever-blooming flower-bed.
Unspoiled by crowds, unvexed by care —
(Goodness! do hear the urchin swear.)

How soft the summer showers fall,
On field and garden, cheering all;
How bright in woods the diamond sheen,
Of rain-drops strung on threads of green —
Each oak a king with jewel crown.
(The wind has blown the hay-stack down!
I knew 'twould hail, it got so warm.
That fence is flat. My! what a storm!)

How soft the hazy summer night!
On dewy grass the moon's pale light
Rests dreamily. It falls in town,
On smoky roofs and pavements brown.
How tenderly when night is gone,
Breaks o'er the fields the summer dawn!
How sweet and pure the scented morn.
(Get up! Old Molly's in the corn!)

Far from the city's dust and broil,
We women sing at household toil,
Nor scorn to work with hardened hands;
We laugh at fashion's bars and bands,

And on our cheeks wear nature's rose.
(That calf is nibbling at my clothes!
Off she goes at double shuffle,
Chewing down my finest ruffle!)

We workers in our loom of life,
Far from the city's din and strife,
Weave many a soft, poetic rose,
With patient hand through warp of prose;
We love our labor more and more.
(John! here! the pigs are at the door!
They 've burst the sty and scaled the wall—
There goes my kettle, soap and all!)

MRS. ALLERTON.

ONLY A NEGRO.

(NOTE.—Harry and Millie Pembleton, husband and wife, were educated octoroons, he being a slave, while she was a free girl. When the Black Law of Arkansas was enacted, in 1857, providing for the expulsion of all free negroes from the State unless they returned into slavery, Millie and her little daughter, Marcia, fled to Kansas. Through the trials that she underwent, Millie became almost insane, and would sit for hours brooding over the hope that was nearest her heart, often seeing vain visions of Harry by her side. Harry finally gained his freedom and came to her near the beginning of the Civil War.)

One day, Millie sat as usual talking with Marcia. Her vision had appeared, and Marcia's question had dispelled it.

"What makes you so strange, Mother?" the little girl asked, looking anxiously into the woman's face.

"I don't know, dear one, I don't know. I cannot tell. I don't know, unless I am losing my mind," Millie answered, shuddering.

"Oh, mother!" the girl cried with apparent anguish.

"There he comes again," the woman exclaimed. "Why must the dream torment me so? No," she continued, "it

is not Harry. My fancy is too wild. No, Harry was a
sound man. This is a poor cripple. Yet it is Harry's face,
his step — but only one arm! He is near. Marcia, do
you see a man coming! Who is he?"

A tall, muscular form strode toward them. Before
Marcia answered, he stopped and raised his right hand,
the only remaining one, to shade his eyes, while he
stared at the woman and her daughter.

"It is Millie," he muttered. "Millie! Marcia!" he
cried.

Millie sprang suddenly up, forgetting her weight of sorrow. Some of the old beauty returned to her face as she
threw herself upon her husband's neck.

"Is this only a dream?" she cried. "Must I wake to
regret this again? Are you really come, Harry? But
where is your arm? It is off at the elbow."

"That is half the price of my liberty," he said.

"How did you do it, papa?" asked Marcia.

"A gun-shot did it," he replied. Looking into his wife's
face, he continued: "There was war all around me. And
when I heard of you and Marcia here in Kansas, needing
me every day to protect you, it was easy to make up my
mind to do it. Almost before I knew it, it was done. I
was worthless to Master, then, and he would soon no doubt
have been glad to get rid of feeding me by giving me freedom. But I could n't wait, and I have brought a hundred
dollars back with me."

He had shot his arm off with his master's musket, in
order to buy his freedom — not just because he desired to
be free, but because Millie and his little daughter needed
him. Heroic soul! that was more than to die for them;
it was to suffer for them.   CARL BRANN.

TELL ME, YE KANSAS WINDS.

Tell me, ye Kansas winds,
    That round my pathway blow,
Is there nowhere a spot
    Where mortal man may go —
No island in the sea,
    No quiet foreign clime,
Where spring-time comes without
    The dire house-cleaning time?
A cyclone struck me with terrific blow,
And hurled me forty rods, as it responded, "No."

Oh, gentle birds that wing
    Far to the south your flight,
Do you not know some land
    Of loveliness and light,
Where beds are never sunned,
    And carpets are not "beat,"
Where "stretchers" are not known,
    And tacks do n't prick your feet?
A large dark bird then flew off with a "Caw,"
And answered with a gruff, disdainful "Naw."

And thou, resplendent moon,
    Pale Empress of the night,
In whose mellifluous beams
    All lovers take delight,
Do you not know a place,
    Some country east or west,

Where from house-cleaning, man,
    Poor man, can get a rest?
The moon then paler grew, and answered slow,
As from behind a cloud it whispered, "No."

Oh, sweetener of my joys,
    My other, better self,
Thou who hast sworn to share,
    My poverty or pelf,
Do you not know some spot,
    On seen or unseen shore,
Where these house-cleaning days
    Shall come again no more?
"Yes, yes," she said, "these tacks here must be
    driven.
You'll find that place sometime — perhaps — in
    heaven."   J. M. Cavaness.

DON'T WAKEN THE BABY.

(Note.—The following lines were formed in my mind when looking at a picture on a writing-tablet cover — a baby asleep in a hammock — its hand hanging over the side, and a playful kitten catching at the little hand. High up in the tree overhead a bird says, "My Sweetest Song I've been Singing.")

My sweetest song I've been singing
    To the baby under the tree,
And the winds' soft hands have been swinging
    And rocking her cradle for me.

And kitty, now you have come creeping,
    In your sly and treacherous way,
To waken and set her a-weeping
    For the dreams you are driving away.

O kitty, do n't waken the baby,
  Let her wander in dreamland away;
For a time is coming when may be
  She will not dream as to-day;

When trouble will sorely perplex her,
  And the little demons of care
Her pillow will haunt, and will vex her
  And sprinkle the snow in her hair.

Then kitty, do n't waken the baby,
  Let her slumber in peace while she may;
For a time is coming when may be
  She will not sleep as to-day.

Mrs. S. N. Wood.

MY AMBITION.

I have my own ambition.   It is not
  To mount on eagles' wings and soar away
Beyond the palings of the common lot,
  Scorning the griefs and joys of every day;
I would be human, toiling like the rest,
  With tender, human heart-beats in my breast.

Not on cold, lonely heights, above the ken
  Of common mortals, would I build my fame,
But in the kindly hearts of living men.
  There, if permitted, would I write my name;
Who builds above the clouds must dwell alone—
  I count good-fellowship above a throne.

And so beside my door I sit and sing
  My simple strains, now sad, now light and gay;
Happy if this or that but wake one string
  Whose low, sweet echoes give me back the lay;
And happier still if, girded by my song,
    Some strained and tempted soul stands firm and
      strong.

Humanity is much the same; if I
  Can give my neighbor's pent-up thought a tongue,
And can give voice to his unspoken cry
  Of bitter pain, when my own heart is wrung,
Then we two meet upon a common land,
  And henceforth stand together, hand in hand.

I send my thought its kindred thought to greet,
  Out to the far frontier, through crowded town.
Friendship is precious, sympathy is sweet;
  So these be mine I ask no laurel crown.
Such my ambition, which I here unfold;
  So it be granted, mine is wealth untold.

Mrs. Allerton.

CHILDHOOD.

It passed in beauty,
  Like the waves that reach
Their jeweled fingers
  Up the sanded beach.

·It passed in beauty,
  Like the flowers that spring
Behind the footsteps
  Of the Winter King.

It passed in beauty,
  Like the clouds on high,
That drape the ceilings
  Of a summer sky.   IRONQUILL.

PILGRIM BARD.

To whom the green sward is like bed of down,
  With no pavilion save the starlit sky,
Upon whose locks the evening dews have shown ;
Who often slept among the wilds alone,
  The while the coyotes sing his lullaby.

Gladly would I backward turn Time's mystic wheel,
  And make this land again a desert wild ;
I care not what the future may reveal ;
  But memories of the past will o'er me steal —
Again I would be nature's reckless child.

                              SCOTT CUMMINS.

TO-DAY.

Work on, work on —
  Work wears the world away ;
Hope when to-morrow comes,
  But work to-day.

Work on, work on —
 Work brings its own relief;
He who most idle is
 Has most grief.

IRONQUILL.

"OLD JIM."

A TRUE STORY FOR BOYS.

Early in the morning of the 12th of April, 1860, on Cedar creek, a tributary of the Cottonwood river, in the southeastern portion of the Territory of Kansas, might have been seen a small boy scampering as fast as his short legs would carry him toward a log cabin that stood in the bend of the creek, under the protecting branches of a large leaning black walnut tree.

Was he running to tell of the approach of a hostile band of Indians, or that a herd of buffaloes or a flock of wild turkeys were in sight?

No; Indian scares were frequent, and buffaloes and wild turkeys were seen so often as to scarcely cause remark.

This curly-headed boy, whom we will call Dick — because that was not his real name — was the bearer of far more interesting news, and arriving at the cabin with eyes wide open and cheeks aglow, he breathlessly announced, "Old Fanny has a colt!"

What attraction had the partially finished breakfast of corn bread and buffalo steak for the three other juvenile members of the family? All rushed pell-mell to see the wonder, with father and mother more leisurely bringing up the rear.

Sure enough, there stood old Fanny, the family horse, quietly cropping the grass, and anon turning her head to look fondly at the wonder—a mealy-nosed, sleek, long-legged bay colt.

Many were the encomiums passed by the children on his bright eyes, sleek coat, and curly mane and tail.

I doubt whether Stanley, with his three hundred followers, made a more thoroughly beaten path through the jungles of Africa than was made by the children from the cabin to the little inclosure during the three ensuing days.

The colt was named "Jim" by Dick; and brother and sisters, father and mother, and even old Fanny, seemed to acquiesce in the decision.

Jim received his christening the third day after his birth in this wise: He had learned to exercise his long legs by running in a circle around his mother, daily enlarging it, as his strength and speed increased. Notwithstanding the admonitory whinnyings of old Fanny and the earnest solicitations of Dick, he would run dangerously near the creek bank, till, alas! an unlucky turn sent him rolling over a twenty-foot bank into the creek.

Simultaneously fell all that seemed worth having to the boy Dick.

To run to the cabin, report the catastrophe, and return with the whole family to the rescue, was the work of a few moments. Dick peered over the bank and saw Jim, with ears laid back, and his body almost submerged in the water, clinging to a shallow slope. Father descended with rope in hand, and secured it around the colt's body, and, with the assistance of all hands, pulled him up, and Dick's pride lay meekly stretched on the grass to dry. Rubbed over, laughed over and cried over betimes, he

was soon on his feet, and as ready for another race — but
not near that bank. Colts, like boys, must sometimes
learn from bitter experience.

This year came the excessive drouth and "festive"
grasshoppers to destroy the crops. The grass which the
year before would hide Dick from view while sitting on
the back of old Fanny, was so short that it could not be
cut with a scythe. As a consequence, Jim and his mother
had to live through that severe winter of cold and snow,
on buds of trees, called "browse," which Dick and his
father cut down so the horses and cattle could get at
them.

When Jim became a full-grown horse, with muscles of
iron, sinews of whalebone, and a constitution that nothing
seemed to impair or fatigue, old men would say, with a
knowing shake of the head, "It is because he was not
pampered while young."

When Jim was a year and a half old, Old Fanny's mate
died, and Jim was hitched with his mother to draw pump-
kins, corn and hay; when two, he helped to do the spring
plowing, and in the fall, Dick, with a pair of revolvers,
made his first run after buffaloes, bringing down three
before he stopped.

Though scarcely three years old, he was known, far and
near, as "Old Jim," and whether running races against
the ponies of friendly Indians, pulling loads of corn to
distant points on the overland Santa Fé route, returning
through snow-drifts with a load of buffalo meat, or, by his
speed and endurance, saving Dick's curly head from the
Indian's scalping-knife, "Old Jim's" mealy nose always
came out in the lead.

It is no wonder that Old Jim became an expert swimmer, since his practice commenced at the age of three days. Before the close of the first summer of his life Dick taught him to have no fear of water, by at first leading him beyond his depth and compelling him to swim out; and later, while hunting cows, swimming old Fanny across the creek at every opportunity, and of course Jim would follow. In those days people often had to go fifteen or twenty miles after their mail, the person going bringing the mail for the whole neighborhood. Dick and Old Jim made this journey when streams were high. In swimming the first stream on the return trip Jim missed his footing in entering the creek, and horse, rider and mail went topsy-turvy into the water. After landing on the opposite side, Dick informed Old Jim that as he was to blame for the present moist condition of the three — the horse, the rider, and the mail — he should swim every ravine and creek between that place and home, and they did. Paying no regard to roads, banks, or crossings, they made a direct line for home, arriving much sooner than they would — Old Jim suffering not a whit. But the sad plight of Dick and the mail! It took much turning and drying by the large chimney-fire to make Dick comfortable and to get the letters and papers in a readable condition.

Would you like to hear of Old Jim's and Dick's race with the Indians?

Well, it happened in this wise: When Jim was five years old and Dick was fourteen, he rode Jim up the valley in search of some ponies that had strayed or been stolen by Indians.

The Indians were known to be hostile, and were reported near. Dick, seated on faithful Old Jim, with a navy revolver under each elbow, felt quite bold, and a match for three or four Indians at the least; but he felt quite differently after a fruitless search of several hours, when within three miles of home he observed, a few miles south, a band of twenty savages, five or six of whom started to cut off his retreat toward the house. Dick was scared—there was no gainsaying that! Though he was well armed, and could shoot as well as the Indians of the plains, he now realized that he was not a match for a half-dozen red-skins. But his confidence in the speed and endurance of Old Jim was unbounded, and these he proceeded to put to the test. As Jim began to feel the excitement of the chase, Dick prudently held him with a steady rein, knowing he would need the horse's best efforts at the last.

Dick has the farthest to go, but has the advantage in knowing by-paths and creek-crossings. He can see the Indians, confident now of a scalp to adorn their belt, riding at a break-neck gait, whenever he or the Indians cross over an eminence. Dick crosses the creek for the last time, half a mile from the cabin, and now has to cross an open prairie. The Indians are now behind the hill. With flying mane and red nostrils spread, Old Jim soon covers the distance, and dashes up to the cabin just as the Indians make their appearance over the brow of the hill.

The Indians proved to be a band of roving Kickapoos, who had been on a thieving expedition into the Cherokee country, and whether they wished to murder Dick and steal his horse, or whether they did it to frighten him, as was their custom when they found one alone on the prairies, will never be known. Certain it is, however, that Dick yet delights to tell how, when a boy, Old Jim saved his scalp; and it is equally certain that from this day Jim was more than ever a favorite with the whole family.

Jim was faithful, willing, and as we before observed, as "tough as a knot." Many were the good offers in ponies, cattle and hard cash for him, but the whole family were unanimous in the conclusion that Old Jim was a permanent fixture in the family, and should remain as long as he lived. But alas! how uncertain are we to carry out our best resolutions.

Jim has become an old horse — seventeen — Dick a man with full beard. Poor Old Jim was again put to the test, but to fail, and the pride of horse and master humbled. After an absence from home at school Dick returned, and, with Old Jim and his mate hitched to a covered wagon, started with several others on a buffalo hunt, south of the Chikaskia river. Buffalo were wild and scarce, water on the prairies plentiful; hence the buffalo would not come to the creek to drink where the hunter lay in wait to shoot them. Dick decided to make a run on Old Jim. But, alas, for the result! Whether because of the increased weight of the rider, or the increased age of Old Jim, or both, they failed to come alongside of the bison as of yore; and, during the exciting chase, Dick inadvertently put a pistol bullet into his own leg instead of a buffalo. An hour after, they came into camp, Dick looking pale from loss of blood, and Old Jim looking tired and crestfallen, and seeming to say, "I did my best, but I am not so young and spry as I used to be."

Time passes. Old Jim is twenty-two. Faithful and honest yet, but quite feeble at times, and good only at slow work. With age he has learned several things that an observant horse is sure to do. He is liable to slip the halter and be found at the oat-bin. He has learned to watch for an open gate into the orchard or stack-lot, and to kick up his heels defiantly at those who try to head him off. He will not always submit to being caught in the morning, but toward evening he will come to the gate and stand for hours. He sometimes concludes that small boys who jerk the reins do not know how to plow corn, and, after tramping down a square rod of corn, will come to the house dragging the shovel-plow in spite of the small boy's tugging at the lines.

Should you with a small switch begin to chastise him for some of his tricks he will utter the most heart-rending groans, as if the punishment were causing excruciating pain.

Old Jim never became confused nor lost his way after dark, but after his rider had given up and concluded to let Jim have his way, notwithstanding he seemed to be going the opposite direction from the right one, he invariably came out at the right place—home.

Old Jim is past twenty-three years old. Dick has left the old homestead, and Father and other members of the family, including Old Jim, have moved to the village. No broad prairies, nor orchard-lot containing sweet clover or timothy for Old Jim. He chafes and does not thrive under this village treatment.

The drayman has offered a liberal price for him, but Dick's father pictures Old Jim shivering on the streets of a stormy day, or struggling with a load too heavy for his now enfeebled condition. No; Jim must not be sold to the drayman nor turned out to die, since he has served so faithfully.

But friends and circumstances at last prevail: Old Jim is sold to a kind master who goes to the Neosho Valley to gather corn. His mealy nose is turned from home for the last time; with ears pricked forward, he starts for the land of corn and clover hay, where, let us hope, he lived several years and died among friends which he was sure to make in his new home.

What became of Dick? Well, excuse me; my story was of Old Jim.

F. H. B.

QUOTATIONS.

"Each has his work and way,
Each has his part and play,
Each has his task to do.
    Both of the good and true,
Though thou art grave and gay,
    Be thou yet brave and true.

"Work for the right and just,
With an intrepid trust;
Then it need matter thee
Not that thou buried be,
Either on land or strand,
Either 'neath soil or sea."

—*From Ware's "Child of Fate."*

"It 's the duty of the poet,
    It 's the duty of the statesman,
To inspire a Nation's life with noble aims;
    And dishonor will o'ershadow
    Him who dare not, or who falsely,
His immortal-fruited mission misproclaims."

—*From Ware's "Decoration Day."*

" To-day our choicest colors are unfurled;
　Soar up, proud bird, and circle 'round the world,
　And we predict that nowhere will you find
　A place like Kansas that you left behind.
　He who has lived in Kansas, though he roam,
　Can find no other spot and call it ' Home.' "

　　　　　—From Ware's "Corn Poem."

" Hope's idle dreams the real vainly follows,
　Facts stay as fadeless as the Parthenon,
　While fancies, like the summer-tinted swallows,
　Flit gayly 'mid its arches and are gone."

　　　　　—From Ware's "The Real."

" They call Kansas the Sunflower State. Not because it is overrun with the noxious weed, but because as the sunflower turns on its stem to catch the first beams of the morning sun, and with its broad disk and yellow rays follows the great orb of day, so Kansas turns to catch the first rays of every advancing thought, or civilized agency, and with her broad prairies and golden fields welcomes and follows the light." *—Charles F. Scott.*

"To rest as well as labor
　God made both brawn and brain,
　And strongest brain and muscle
　Endure not ceaseless strain.
　Let once the springs be broken,
　The loss is great indeed :
　Work, then, but labor wisely,
　And thine be labor's need."

　　　　　—Mrs. Allerton.

"AD ASTRA PER ASPERA."

" O'er rugged rocks to starry skies,
   By prickly paths to thrones on high;
   Through grief to glory — is the cry."

— W. H. Bradbury.

AL FRISCO.

" Grand 'Out-of-Doors,' impartial temple, where
   No elevated stage nor seats reserved
   Give preference; open and free alike for all,
   With walls thrown down and roof blown off,
   Is Nature's panorama here unrolled."

— W. H. Bradbury.

"Though border war her cities overrun,
   Though swarms of locusts shade the summer sun,
   No matter what misfortunes may occur,
   The State goes on as if they never were.
   Cities arise where towns were burned before,
   The prairies sparkle with the church and store,
   And painted harvesters, fleet after fleet,
   Like yachts, career through seas of waving wheat."

" When other orators, in other verse,
   Far better days in better ways rehearse,
   When other crowds composed of other men,
 · Shall re-enact the present scenes again,
   May they be able then to say that she
   Is all that we have wished the State to be."

—From Ware's "Corn Poem."

"The world is but an ocean of unrest,
  Whose tidal billows wander to the West.
  For age on age the ancient East did hold
  Unnumbered people and uncounted gold.

"Most happy Kansas! prosperous and free,
  She rests upon the margin of the sea;
  And day by day upon her shores are hurled
  The tidal billows of the olden world."
            —*From Ware's "Short-Haired Poet."*

"As the strings of a harp, standing side by side,
  Are the days of sadness and days of song;
The sunshine and shadows are ever allied,
But the shadows will fade and the sun abide,
    Though to-day may be dim and the world go wrong."
            —*From Ware's "Shadow."*

KANSAS SYMPOSIUM.

With freedom's barriers broken down—with eye of faith
    grown dim,
Thou wast for battling cause of right—watchword and
    synonym!
Again—in nation's darkest hour—when through her open
    gate
The trait'rous host came rushing out, thou pressed in,
    true State!
By night a pillared cloud of fire, by day a shining sun;
"Ad astra per aspera"—always thou leadest on.
            —*B. W. Woodward, Lawrence.*

Not for what she has done for me,
    Though it be great;
For what she is, her majesty,
    I love my state.

—*Thomas Emmet Dewey, Abilene.*

The most remarkable thing about Kansas, from '54 to
'91, has been its courage and moral leadership.

—*D. W. Wilder, Hiawatha.*

Thine is the land where the swift-flying shadows
    Wander at will o'er monotonous plains;
Kiss the fresh blossoms that spangle the meadows,
    And sail o'er seas of voluptuous grains.
Dear are thy childings and sweet thy caresses,
    Tender thy eyes where the warm love-light broods;
Bright is the sunlight amid thy soft tresses,
    Loving thy heart, but inconstant thy moods.

—*George C. Sperry, Topeka.*

Kansas, most loved of Fortune's guests,
    Child of our hopes and fears—
Kansas, whose genius ever wrests
    Victory from Failure's tears—
Thy children hail thee as the best,
    And will for ceaseless years.

—*J. W. D. Anderson, Elk City.*

I have known Kansas thirty-one years, as a Territory
and as a State, in war and in peace, in famine and in

plenty, and I have never known a man who trusted and believed in her, and in evil times waited and hoped for better, who was disappointed or deceived. Those who have known Kansas longest love her most.

—Caroline E. Prentis, Newton.

Of all the States, but three shall live in story:
   Old Massachusetts with her Plymouth rock,
   And old Virginia with her noble stock,
And sunny Kansas with her woes and glory—
These three will live in song and oratory,
   While all the others with their idle claims
   Will only be remembered as mere names.

—E. F. Ware, Fort Scott.

AN ACROSTIC.

Kansas! Fair State, we well may claim
   A meed of praise for thee;
None other boasts so great a fame,
   So grand a history,
As through oppressions, strifes and wars
She soars triumphant to the stars.

—Maggie Kilmer, Sedan.

KANSAS HEROES.

Not best the stretching fields of golden grain,
The harvest plenitude of fertile plain;
'Twas not for these they struck the effectual blow
That broke the power of a malignant foe.
Their blood for Freedom shed must consecrate
To human Liberty this sovereign State.

—Allen D. Gray, Topeka.

KISMET.

A word doth make our destiny.   We bravely said
Ad Astra, when the night engulfed our martyred dead;
And when the morning flushed the pallid eastern sky,
Our chosen character was registered on high.

     —Florence L. Snow, Neosho Falls.

CRADLE OF FREEDOM.

Men said — a noble few — that Kansas soil
Should yield its fruitage but to freemen's toil;
And Freedom, cradled here, grown great and strong,
Rose in her might to cope with ancient wrong.
"Set free! set free!" she cried, nor stayed her hand
Till only crime wore chains in all the land.

     —Ellen P. Allerton, Padonia.

KANSAS, '56–'90.

Drenched with impetuous martyr blood she stands
 A nation's pride — the weeping cynosure
Of all the world.   Deflowered by ruthless hands,
 Defamed, dishonored, reft of all that's pure,
  To rise a spotless monument, at last,
  For all the future and to all the past.

     —Albert Bigelow Paine, Fort Scott.

THE NATION'S GARDEN.

Its arid wastes shall verdant be;
 With golden harvests shall they gleam.
Its verdant plains shall peopled be.
 The nation's garden yet shall teem,
  Not with the flower of chivalry,
  But with a free and noble yeomanry.

     —Wm. H. Tibbals.

The wretched slave whose galling chains the gods
　Dared not to break, turned in his mute despair
To Kansas, and she struck for him a blow
　That swelled into a universal prayer,
　　Till o'er the tomb of slavery rose a star
　　Of freedom, shining through the clouds of war!
　　　　　　　　　— *Will Lisenbee, Cherokee.*

O Kansas!　Land where poets sing
　Of freedom, health, and homes of peace;
Where from the furrowed acres spring
　A wealth for all the world's increase;
　　Where honor, worth and truth are prized,
　　And fondest hopes are realized.
　　　　　　　—Al. M. Hendee, Kansas City.

Kansas is freedom's birth-place, glory's pathway, chivalry's temple, the home of patriotism.　A land whose boundless plains and deathless waters have witnessed the dawn of fame.　　　　*—Lizzie B. Hamrick.*

Kansas, how sublime thy story,
Crowning of a nation's glory,
First in all our hearts forever.
First the slave's curs'd bonds to sever,
　With thy temperance banner o'er us,
Bright the future's sheen before us.
　　　　　—Laura E. Newell, Zeandale, Kansas.

ABOVE CRITICISM.

My love, much praised, much blamed, grows moody quite,
    The good words fail to drive away the ill;
But Kansas, blessed, maligned, shows no affright,
    Instead, moves nobly on, unruffled still —
        Serenely sure, unminding wreaths of scars,
        Firm-stepped, she mounts her pathway to the stars.
                —Chas. Moreau Harger, Abilene.

        Kansas, like thy favorite flower,
          Has thy race, thus far, been run;
        Morning, evening, finds thee facing
          Towards the right's progressive sun.
              — Sol. T. Long, Grenola.

Kansas is the nation's political experiment farm.   Reforms admitted to be desirable, but of doubtful practicability, are first tried in Kansas.   If they fail here the experiment is carried no farther.
          —Chas. F. Scott, Iola.

KANSAS SKIES.

If Grecian skies inspired Grecian bards to sing
The melodies that still adown the ages ring —
If skies inspire, ye Kansas Bards, lift up your eyes;
How rare must be the verse to match the Kansas skies.
        —Ida A. Ahlborn, Baldwin.

When Freedom's banner is unfurled,
    No star among its folds of blue
Shines forth to Nations far and wide
    With luster brighter, with beams more true;

Tho' oft mid clouds 'tis hidden quite —
It rises ever for the right.

           —Ida Capen Fleming, El Dorado.

As knight of old, alone, before the fray,
Rode out to meet his boldest foe midway,

Met, strove and conquered in the army's sight,
And came with trophy worthy of the fight —

So thou, my State, return, thy Leader greet,
And lay a broken wine-glass at his feet.

           —Hattie Horner, Whitewater.

Child of the grassy plain,
    Facing the day,
Blooming in sun or rain,
    Evermore gay,
Coming the first to bless,
    Wide-spreading wilderness,
Flaunting and free ;
    Coming in power,
Kansas is like to thee,
    Sunflower.   *—Noble L. Prentis.*

I love thee, Home-land, when I pass
In western wilds, through wind-tossed grass ;
And yet more dearly when I spy
Thy rosy children, romping by ;

But yet of all I count this best —
Thy moral honor, east and west.

           —Mrs. L. E. Thrope, Topeka.

PART III.

MISCELLANEOUS.

MISCELLANEOUS.

KANSAS.

There were no white inhabitants of Kansas in 1850. In 1856 there were less than 10,000. In 1860 there were 107,000. In 1861 she was admitted into the Union. In 1880 there were 996,000 inhabitants within her borders. In 1890 there were probably not less than two millions. From the Missouri State line on the east to the Colorado line on the west, from the 37th to the 40th degrees of north latitude, the land is filled with a happy and a prosperous and a virtuous people. There is a church in every hamlet, a school-house on every hillock, and the golden, tangled maize waves its amber locks in the summer breezes, where the buffalo wallowed and the coyote drank. The crack of the hunter's rifle has given place to the chime of the church-bell, and the smoke from half a million happy firesides has replaced the solitary trapper's fire. Where the Indian scalped his enemy the clergyman preaches Christ, and the war-dance of the aborigines has retired before the communion table of the Christian. Where the beaver built his dam the saw and grist mill now stand, and populous cities, rich in all the fruits of the nineteenth century civilization, occupy the former sites of the prairie-dog villages.

Westward the star of empire has indeed taken its way, and its brightest beams are thrown with most effulgent splendor over the magnificent area of Kansas.

— National Tribune.

LE MARAIS DU CYGNE.

A blush as of roses
   Where rose never grew !
Great drops on the bunch-grass,
   But not of the dew !
A taint in the sweet air
   For wild bees to shun !
A stain that shall never
   Bleach out in the sun !

Back, steed of the prairies !
   Sweet song-bird, fly back !
Wheel hither, bald vulture !
   Gray wolf, call thy pack !
The foul human vultures
   Have feasted and fled ;
The wolves of the Border
   Have crept from the dead.

In the homes of their rearing,
   Yet warm with their lives,
Ye wait the dead only,
   Poor children and wives !
Put out the red forge-fire,
   The smith shall not come ;
Unyoke the brown oxen,
   The plowman lies dumb.

Wind slow from the Swan's Marsh,
   O dreary death-train,
With pressed lips as bloodless
   As lips of the slain !

Kiss down the young eyelids,
  Smooth down the gray hairs;
Let tears quench the curses
  That burn through your prayers.

From the hearths of their cabins,
  The fields of their corn,
Unwarned and unweaponed,
  The victims were torn —
By the whirlwind of murder
  Swooped up and swept on
To the low, reedy fen-lands,
  The Marsh of the Swan.

With a vain plea for mercy
  No stout knee was crooked;
In the mouths of the rifles
  Right manly they looked.
How paled the May sunshine,
  Green Marais du Cygne,
When the death-smoke blew over
  Thy lonely ravine!

Strong man of the prairies,
  Mourn bitter and wild!
Wail, desolate woman!
  Weep, fatherless child!
But the grain of God springs up
  From ashes beneath,
And the crown of His harvest
  Is life out of death.

Not in vain on the dial
  The shade moves along
To point the great contrasts
  Of right and of wrong ;
Free homes and free altars
  And fields of ripe food ;
The reeds of the Swan's Marsh,
  Whose bloom is of blood.

On the lintels of Kansas
  That blood shall not dry ;
Henceforth the Bad Angel
  Shall harmless go by ;
Henceforth to the sunset,
  Unchecked on her way,
Shall Liberty follow
  The march of the day.

JOHN G. WHITTIER.

THE BURIAL OF BARBER.

Frozen earth to frozen breast,
Lay your slain one down to rest ;
  Lay him down in hope and faith ;
And above the broken sod,
Once again to Freedom's God
  Pledge yourselves for life or death —

That the State whose walls ye lay,
In your blood and tears to-day,
  Shall be free from bonds of shame,

And your goodly land untrod
By the feet of slavery, shod
  With cursing as with flame.

Plant the buckeye on his grave,
For the hunter of the slave
  In its shadows cannot rest;
And let martyr mound and tree
Be your pledge and guarantee
  Of the freedom of the West.
WHITTIER.

THE KANSAS EMIGRANT'S SONG.
TUNE— *"Auld Lang Syne."*

(NOTE.—This poem was printed in the first issue of the *Herald of Freedom*, one of
the first Free-State papers printed in Kansas, under date of October 21st, 1854.)

We cross the prairies as of old
  The pilgrims crossed the sea,
To make the West, as they the East,
  The homestead of the free.

CHORUS:

The homestead of the free, my boys,
  The homestead of the free;
To make the West, as they the East,
  The homestead of the free.

We go to rear a wall of men
  On Freedom's Southern line,
And plant beside the cotton tree
  The rugged Northern pine!
Chorus.

We 're flowing from our native hills,
  As our free rivers flow;
The blessing of our mother-land
  Is on us as we go.
          Chorus.

We go to plant her common schools
  On distant prairie swells,
And give the Sabbaths of the wild
  The music of her bells.
          Chorus.

Upbearing, like the ark of old,
  The Bible in our van,
We go to test the truth of God
  Against the fraud of man.
          Chorus.

No pause, nor rest, save where the streams
  That feed the Kansas run,
Save where our pilgrim gonfalon
  Shall flout the setting sun.
          Chorus.

We 'll sweep the prairies as of old
  Our fathers swept the sea,
And make the West, as they the East,
  The homestead of the free.
          Chorus.
                              WHITTIER.

K T DID.

(AN EARLY POEM.)

From her borders far away,
Kansas blows a trumpet call,
Answered by the loud "Hurrah!"
Of her troopers one and all,
Knife and pistol, sword and spur.
Cries K T —
"Let my troopers all concur,
To the old flag no demur —
Follow me!"
Hence the song of jubilee;
Platy Phillis from the tree,
High among the branches hid,
Sings all night merrily,
        K T did
    She did — she did.

Thirty score Jayhawkers bold,
Kansas men of strong renown,
Rally round the banner old,
Casting each his gauntlet down.
"Good for Kansas!" one and all
        Cry to her;
Riding to her trumpet call,
Blithe as to a festival,
        All concur.
Hence the revel and the glee,
As the chanter from the tree,

High among the branches hid,
Sings all night so merrily,
    K T did,
She did — she did.
        —From N. Y. Vanity Fair.

PROPHETIC WORDS OF SUMNER,

On the Passage of the Kansas and Nebraska Bill.

"In passing this bill as it is now threatened, you scatter from this dark midnight hour no seeds of harmony and good-will, but broadcast through the land dragon's-teeth which haply may spring up in direful crops of armed men; but yet I am assured, sir, they will fructify in civil strife and feud.   Sir, the bill which you are about to pass is at once the worst and the best bill on which Congress ever acted.

"It is the *worst* bill, inasmuch as it is a present victory for Slavery.   Sir, it is the *best* bill on which Congress ever acted, for it annuls all compromises with Slavery, and makes all future compromises impossible.   Thus it puts Freedom and Slavery face to face, and bids them grapple. Who can doubt the result ?   Thus, sir, now standing at the very grave of Freedom in Nebraska and Kansas, I lift myself to that happy resurrection by which Freedom will be secured, not only in these Territories, but everywhere under the National Government.   Sorrowfully I bend before the wrong which you are about to commit. Joyfully I welcome all the promises of the future."

WORDS OF WARREN WILKES, OF SOUTH CAROLINA,

ON THE KANSAS AND NEBRASKA BILL.

"By consent of parties, the present contest in Kansas is made the turning-point in the destinies of Slavery and Abolitionism. If the South triumphs, Abolitionism will be defeated and shorn of its power for all time. If she is defeated, Abolitionism will grow more insolent and aggressive, until the utter ruin of the South is consummated. If the South secures Kansas, she will extend slavery into all the territory south of the 40th parallel of north latitude to the Rio Grande; and this, of course, will secure for her pent-up institution of Slavery an ample outlet, and restore her power in Congress. If the North secures Kansas, the power of the South in Congress will be gradually diminished. The States of Missouri, Kentucky, Tennessee, Arkansas, and Texas, together with the adjacent Territories, will gradually become Abolitionized, and the slave population confined to the States east of the Mississippi will become valueless. *All depends on the action of the present movement.*"

EMERSON ON KANSAS.

"Kings shook with fear.
Old empires crave the secret force to find
  Which fired the little State,
To save the rights of all mankind.

Let the blood of her hundred thousand
Throb in each manly vein,
   And the wit of all her wisest
Make sunshine in her brain;
   And each shall care for other,
And each to each shall bend —
   To the poor a noble brother
To the good an equal friend."

ORIGINAL JOHN BROWN SONG.

("George Ropes gives the *Capital* the real origin of John Brown Song. It arose with Major Ralph Newton's 'Tigers,' the second battalion Massachusetts Volunteer Militia, ordered to Fort Warren, in Boston Harbor, in April, 1861."—[Wilder's Annals.] We insert it because few have ever seen the original song.)

John Brown's body lies a-mouldering in the grave;
John Brown's body lies a-mouldering in the grave;
John Brown's body lies a-mouldering in the grave;
   His soul is marching on.

CHORUS:

Glory, glory, Hallelujah!
Glory, glory, Hallelujah!
Glory, glory, Hallelujah!
   His soul is marching on.

He's gone to be a soldier in the army of the Lord;
He's gone to be a soldier in the army of the Lord;
He's gone to be a soldier in the army of the Lord;
   His soul is marching on.
   Chorus.

John Brown's knapsack is strapped upon his back;
John Brown's knapsack is strapped upon his back;
John Brown's knapsack is strapped upon his back;
　　His soul is marching on.

Chorus.

His pet lambs will meet him on the way;
His pet lambs will meet him on the way;
His pet lambs will meet him on the way,
　　While they go marching on.

Chorus.

Now three rousing cheers for the Union;
Now three rousing cheers for the Union;
Now three rousing cheers for the Union,
　　As we go marching on.

Chorus.

A CALL TO KANSAS.

TUNE—"*Nelly Bly.*"

(In February, 1855, Dr. Thomas H. Webb, secretary of the New England Emigrant
Aid Company, offered a prize of $50 for a Kansas song. Eighty-nine were presented.
The prize was awarded to Lucy Larcom, for "A Call to Kansas.")

Yeomen strong, hither throng!
　　Nature's honest men;
We will make the wilderness.
　　Bud and bloom again.
Bring the sickle, speed the plow,
　　Turn the ready soil!
Freedom is the noblest pay
　　For the true man's toil.

Ho, brothers ! come brothers !
    Hasten all with me ;
We 'll sing upon the Kansas plains
    A song of Liberty.

Father, haste !   O'er the waste
    Lies a pleasant land.
There your fireside's altar-stones,
    Fixed in truth, shall stand.
There your sons, brave and good,
    Shall to freemen grow,
Clad in triple mail of right,
    Wrong to overthrow.
Ho, brothers ! come, brothers !
    Hasten all with me ;
We 'll sing upon the Kansas plains
    A song of Liberty !

Mother, come ! here 's a home
    In the waiting West ;
Bring the seeds of love and peace,
    You who sow them best.
Faithful hearts, holy prayers,
    Keep from taint the air ;
Soil a mother's tears have wet
    Golden crops shall bear.
Come, mother ! fond mother,
    List, we call to thee ;
We 'll sing upon the Kansas plains
    A song of Liberty !

Brother brave, stem the wave !
　Firm the prairies tread !
Up the dark Missouri flood
　Be your canvas spread.
Sister true, join us too,
　Where the Kansas flows ;
Let the Northern lily bloom　·
　With the Southern Rose.
Brave brother ! true sister !
　List, we call to thee ;
We 'll sing upon the Kansas plains
　A song of Liberty !

One and all, hear our call
　Echo through the land !
Aid us with a willing heart
　And the strong right hand !
Feed the spark the Pilgrims struck
　On old Plymouth rock !
To the watch-fires of·the free
　Millions glad shall flock.
Ho, brother ! come, brother !
　Hasten, all, with me ;
We 'll sing upon the Kansas plains
　·A song of Liberty.

POETIC DESCRIPTION.

(The following poetic description of the country included in Kansas Territory as described by Longfellow, is found in F. G. Adams's "Homestead Guide," printed in 1873. "Here is given to the Platte its other designation, the Nebraska, and Fontaine-qui-bout is spoken of as the principal tributary of the Arkansas.")

Far in the West there lies a desert land, where the mount-
    ains
Lift, through perpetual snows, their lofty and luminous
    summits.
Down from their jagged, deep ravines, where the gorge,
    like a gateway,
Opens a passage rude to the wheels of the emigrant's wagon,
Westward the Oregon flows, and the Walleway and
    Owyhee;
Eastward, with devious course, among the Wind river
    mountains,
Through the Sweetwater Valley precipitate leaps the Ne-
    braska;
And to the south, from Fontaine-qui-bout and the Spanish
    sierras;
Fretted with sands and rocks, and swept by the wind of
    the desert,
Numberless torrents, with ceaseless sound, descend to the
    ocean,
Like the great chords of a harp, in loud and solemn vibra-
    tions.
Spreading between these streams are the wondrous, beauti-
    ful prairies,
Billowy bays of grass ever rolling in shadow and sunshine,
Bright with luxuriant clusters of roses and purple amor-
    phas.

Over them wander the buffalo herds, and the elk and the
    roebuck;
Over them wander the wolves, and herds of riderless horses;
Fires that blast and blight, and winds that are weary with
    travel;
Over them wander the scattered tribes of Ishmael's chil-
    dren,
Staining the desert with blood; and above their terrible
    war trails
Circles and sails aloft, on pinions majestic, the vulture,
Like the implacable soul of a chieftain slaughtered in battle,
By invisible stairs ascending and scaling the heavens.
Here and there rise smokes from the camps of these savage
    marauders;
Here and there rise groves from the margins of swift-
    running rivers;
And the grim, taciturn bear, the anchorite monk of the
    desert,
Climbs down their dark ravines to dig for roots by the
    brook-side,
And over all is the sky, the clear and crystalline heaven,
Like the protecting hand of God inverted above them.

www.ingramcontent.com/pod-product-compliance
Lightning Source LLC
Chambersburg PA
CBHW030642030726
47497CB00006B/1915